VEILED VENGEANCE

A SHAYLA MURPHY MYSTERY

STELLA BIXBY

FERRY TAIL PUBLISHING LLC

Cover design by Mariah Sinclair

www.mariahsinclair.com

❀ Created with Vellum

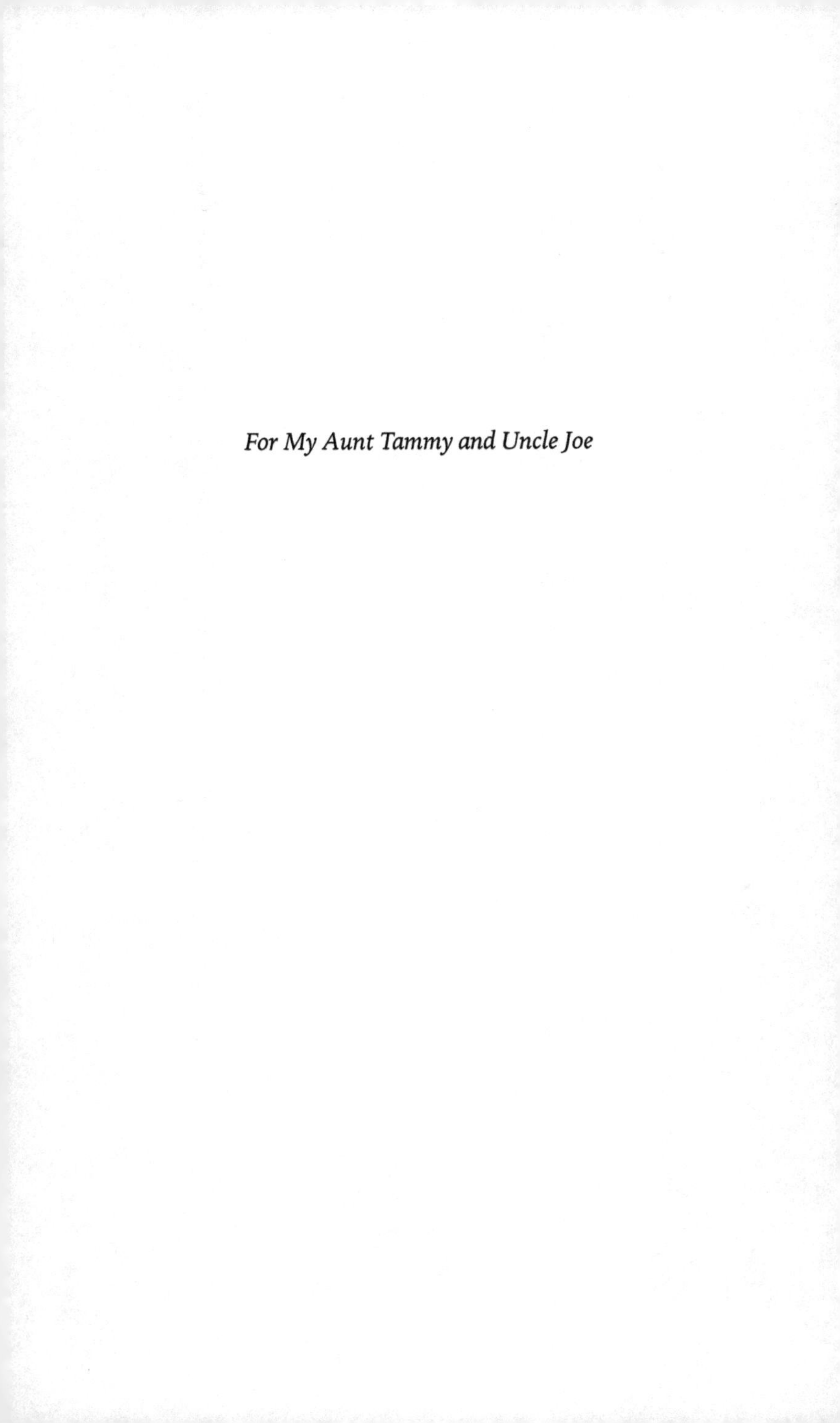

For My Aunt Tammy and Uncle Joe

Thanks to the incoming phone call from my mother, my heart rate skyrocketed. First, my wedding venue planner's call with her urgent meeting request, and now this? What did I do to deserve so much turmoil so early in the morning?

"Yeh don't have to answer it, love," Seamus said in his swoon-worthy Irish brogue. "Yer mam can leave a message."

He was right, but it became a thing whenever I missed my mother's calls.

Like when I was a teenager, and I took a nap after school, causing me to miss several calls from her. Before I knew it, the SWAT team was pounding on the door because she thought someone had broken in and murdered me.

"I'm sure it'll just be a second," I said to Seamus, trying to keep my tone as calm as possible.

I took a deep breath and adjusted my position in the

plushy leather seats of Seamus' fancy car before I answered.

"Hello?" My mom's voice came through the phone before I could say anything. "Shayla, can you hear me? Oh, these stupid international calls. Shayla?"

I put a smile on my face—they said you could hear smiles through the phone—and said, "Hey, Mom. I can hear you loud and clear."

"Then why didn't you say something?"

"I'm sorry. What's going on? Is everything okay?"

"Everything is perfect. Wonderful," she said, though her voice indicated otherwise. "John just told me he's taking me on a year-long worldwide honeymoon after the wedding. Isn't that fantastic?"

"That's great," I said. "I'm sure it'll be fun." John was her fiancé. I'd never met him, but he was the first man she'd actually agreed to marry when he got down on one knee. I felt slightly bad for all the others she'd turned down before John.

"It will be fun." She paused. "I'm calling because I need to make sure you don't schedule your wedding date after August. Unless you're going to wait an entire year to get married."

"Couldn't one of your honeymoon stops be at my wedding?" I asked, gazing out at the parking lot. A bright pink car caught my eye first, then an old, beat-up junker that was entirely out of place among the high-dollar vehicles surrounding it.

"Nothing says buzzkill like spending your honeymoon watching someone else get married," Mom said. "Just schedule it before August, okay?"

I sighed. "I already told you the wedding is in June. We'll be just fine."

"Good. I'll talk to you later."

She hung up before I said goodbye.

Seamus looked at me expectantly.

"She's going on a year-long worldwide honeymoon after her wedding, so we can't move the date past August."

Seamus grabbed my hand and rubbed a thumb over my fingers. "Sure, look, let's focus on our wedding, okay? That will be a wonderful day."

He was right.

Everything would be perfect on our special day.

In June.

"I have some bad news." The venue planner—Patricia—sat stoically behind her desk. A tall, sturdy-looking woman dressed in an all-white uniform with a snake tattoo spiraling up her arm stood off to Patricia's right, holding a clipboard with her eyes narrowed at Seamus and me and another couple sitting next to us.

"Spit it out," the woman next to me said.

"It seems my previous assistant double-booked your weddings." Patricia motioned to the woman next to her. "I assure you, this type of mistake will not happen again."

"What does that mean for us?" Seamus asked, squeezing my hand.

"Because Claudine and Roland scheduled with me

first, they will have the first choice on whether they keep the date or choose another."

I felt my jaw drop as I glared at Patricia. She seemed so cheery, dressed in all pink, from her pink feather earrings to her pink high heels. One of the first lessons I learned in police academy—don't judge a book by its cover.

"We're keeping it," Claudine said without hesitation.

I snuck a peek at her. She and I both had long, blonde, curly hair, but that's where the similarities stopped. She was as thin as a twig, wore designer clothes, and looked like she had one too many encounters with the Botox needle. Her white button-down blouse with its sleeves perfectly cuffed to show off her tanned forearms probably cost twenty times more than the white tank top I wore.

"So be it," Patricia said, closing a notebook in front of her.

The woman standing next to her nodded and made a note on her spreadsheet.

I glanced at the picture on her desk. She stood next to a man with a man bun in front of the Cliffs of Moher. "How would you feel if you and your—uh—" I pointed at the picture.

"Boyfriend," Patricia said.

"You and your boyfriend were told you couldn't have your wedding venue on the planned date? The date you were promised? You'd be devastated." I searched for a solution. "Maybe we can share the day. This place is enormous. I'm sure we could work something out. And then it would cost half as much."

"Money is not an issue for us," Claudine said, standing. "Now that this is settled, I'd like to continue our planning session."

"Hold on," I said. "Can we please discuss this? Do you need the entire venue for the entire twenty-four hours?"

"Yeh can go and bollox if yeh think I'm doing that," Claudine said, her voice completely unapologetic. "It's not me fault yeh booked after me."

I looked back at Patricia. "What are some other dates? Preferably before August?"

Patricia glanced at her computer. "I'm sorry, on such short notice, we have nothing available until November."

She made it sound like I'd just waltzed in and asked to book the venue in less than two months. When, in reality, I'd booked months ago—the moment we set a date.

"Maybe yeh should look for another venue," Claudine said, her Irish voice stuck up and rude.

I wanted to tell her how important this venue was to Seamus—everyone in their family, going back as far as he could remember, had been married inside the renovated castle. Heck, they'd probably been married in the castle before it had been renovated. The location was non-negotiable.

I didn't have the chance to tell her before she and her fiancé walked out of Patricia's office.

I turned back to Patricia. "Are you absolutely certain there aren't any openings before August?"

"Nope, nothing," she said without even looking at her computer screen. "I'm sorry. Maybe we can get you in next summer."

"We won't be waitin' until next summer," Seamus said. "Is there an evening, perhaps?"

Patricia smiled at Seamus. She'd always been slightly shy around him. He had that effect on people. Mainly because he was practically a celebrity in Ireland, as his family was one of the richest on the island. If Ireland had royalty, he would have been the crown prince.

"Even for you, Mr. O'Malley, I can't magically make an opening appear," Patricia said. "Perhaps a longer engagement would be good for you. This might be a sign that you've rushed into things."

Anger flooded me. Was she really trying to tell us what was best for our relationship? I got enough of that talk from my mother. I didn't need it from her too.

Seamus squeezed my hand. "We'll have to discuss our options and get back to yeh."

"Please let me know just as soon as you do. We book up rather quickly." Patricia smiled.

"You know what?" I stood, dropping Seamus' hand, causing the woman at Patricia's side to take a defensive stance. "Whoa, it's okay." I held up my hands. "I just want to talk to Claudine one more time. Maybe if I explain the historical significance of us getting married here, she'll change her mind."

Before either of them could object, I walked out of the office.

2

Ballywick Castle was majestic. Many of the original features were intact or had been remodeled to appear they were. The spiral stone staircases were available for public use, though an elevator had been installed to provide access to each of the five levels—the fifth being the rooftop.

I stood in the center of the main level and glanced up. From that vantage point, I could see all the way to the sky as the center of the castle was open. The other levels also opened to the center with three-hundred-sixty-degree balconies and beautiful wooden railings to keep visitors from falling to their deaths.

An argument echoed from one of the levels above. Maybe Claudine and Roland were having a pre-wedding disagreement. Or maybe he was trying to convince her to let us have the date.

I started up the tight spiral stairway to the second level. This was where Patricia had shown us options for dressing rooms. The wedding would take place on the main level, right in the center of the castle. There was enough room for people to sit in chairs with an aisle down the middle and line the balconies of the second, third, and fourth levels to watch from above. If the day were rainy, they'd stretch a tent over the roof opening to assure the wedding would go on as planned.

My heart fluttered in anticipation. I desperately wanted to get married here. From the moment Seamus mentioned it, I felt a severe sense of duty to my future family. And the moment I saw the castle, I fell in love.

I checked each room on the second level and found no evidence of Claudine or Roland. I tried the third and fourth levels too, but still nothing.

The adrenaline that had overcome me in Patricia's office was wearing off, leaving me out of breath with a hopeless feeling in my gut.

It was no use.

Claudine wouldn't give up her date. She'd made that clear. And she *had* made the reservations before me. It was only fair that she got the venue in June. Seamus and I would just have to wait.

My footsteps made dull thuds as I made my way back down the tight spiral staircase. I'd considered wearing heels but was thankful I hadn't. Even in flats, I had to be careful not to slip on the stone.

I heard someone exclaim something that sounded like, "Ouch!" and then, "What are you talking abooooooooooooouuu!" The scream ended with the unmistakable sound of a body hitting a stone floor. The echoes of the scream and the impact sent chills down my spine.

I hurried as fast as I could down the stairs. It sounded

like other people were rushing to see, too—their heels clicking on the stone steps and echoing up through the stairwell. Once on the second level, I hurried to a balcony and glanced over to find Claudine lying on the stone floor.

Time seemed to slow as I processed what was happening.

Seamus appeared from the direction of Patricia's office, let out a horrific shout, and then rushed to Claudine's body. "Shayla. No. Shayla. Yer okay. Please be okay."

He realized his mistake when he pushed Claudine's ringlets off her face.

"Get off me fiancée, yeh eejit," Roland said, pushing Seamus out of the way and kneeling next to Claudine. "Come on, wake up, love."

Seamus looked confused.

When Patricia appeared from the direction opposite her office—her personal guard assistant closely on her heels—she looked like she was in shock. "What—Claudine—how?" She glanced up and saw me. Recognition washed over her face. "You pushed her!"

I glanced around. Surely, she wasn't talking about me. I looked up at the levels above me. No one else was in her line of sight that I could see.

"You wanted the wedding date so bad you killed off the competition!" Patricia's voice echoed through the castle.

"That's complete bollox," Seamus said. "Shayla would never kill anyone. She's the sweetest person in the entire world."

Panic flooded me. I would never have tried to hurt Claudine. But that was definitely not how it looked.

"I'm calling the Gardaí," Patricia said.

As she raised the phone to her ear, I hurried down the last set of narrow spiral stairs.

My time was limited. I needed to get some photographs of the scene before the Gardaí arrived. Especially since Patricia had already named me as the prime suspect.

Thankfully, I had my phone in my pocket as I'd left my purse in Patricia's office.

"We have a murder here at Ballywick Castle," Patricia said. "The murderer is still on the premises."

I did my best not to roll my eyes.

Seamus hurried up to me and hugged me tightly. "I'm so glad yer all right."

"I'm fine," I said. "But I need to do something really quick."

He released me and whispered, "How can I help?"

"If anyone starts paying attention to me, distract them."

Seamus nodded and moved to Patricia's assistant, who looked like she might pass out at the sight of the crumpled woman on the floor.

Roland was still sobbing at Claudine's side.

I snapped as many photos of Claudine and the surrounding stone as possible, then turned the smartphone lens up at the balcony from where she'd fallen.

When I zoomed in, I could see a touch of blood on the spindles that probably came from Claudine's nose breaking.

I turned back to Claudine and noticed a stain on her shirt sleeve that definitely hadn't been there in Patricia's office.

When I leaned down to take a closer photo, Roland said, "What are you doing?"

I scrambled for an explanation. If I told him I was taking pictures, the gardaí would confiscate my phone.

"I just wanted to check her pulse," I said. "Has anyone confirmed that she's dead?"

Roland looked up at me with a hopeful stare. "Go ahead. Check it."

My insides groaned. Why had I gotten his hopes up? She was obviously dead.

But I had to make it believable.

I reached my fingers down to her neck, finding the carotid artery, and waited.

There were no signs of breathing, though her airway looked clear, minus the broken nose.

I was just about to break Roland's heart for the second time in minutes when I felt it.

A pulse.

"She's still alive."

3

Things moved quickly after that.

The paramedics arrived just after my shocking declaration.

They carefully loaded Claudine onto a stretcher and wheeled her out of the building, with Roland following closely behind.

Amid the chaos, I slipped my phone to Seamus for safekeeping. Patricia and her assistant huddled near the doorway. She shot me a glance every few seconds as if I might run away before the gardaí officers arrived.

"What do you think they're talking about?" I asked Seamus.

"It looks like Patricia is trying to talk her assistant off a ledge, if yeh ask me."

If that's what Patricia was going for, she was failing. The assistant looked even more upset now than when she'd first seen Claudine on the floor. "Poor thing, it must be a challenge working for Patricia. Seeing someone nearly dead is probably the last thing she needs at work."

"She's right over there," Patricia practically yelled when the gardaí walked in. "Don't let her get away."

Molly—followed by several other gardaí—seemed to sigh as she focused her attention on who Patricia was pointing at . . . me.

"You have to be kidding me," she said. "You pushed a woman over a balcony?"

"I didn't," I said. "Of course, I didn't."

Seamus was at my side, rubbing my back.

"I'm sure Molly doesn't actually think yeh did it," Seamus said.

Molly eyed me. I'd venture to guess she wouldn't go easy on me being Seamus' ex-fiancée. I got her out of a sticky situation a few months back and helped her solve a crime not long after. Even so, I was fairly certain she still hated me.

Molly did a quick once-over of the scene before turning her attention back to me.

"Tell me what happened," Molly said. "Walk me through your entire day from the beginning."

She and I had been through similar training. I would bet anything she asked me to go back that far so she could gauge what I sounded and looked like when I was telling the truth versus when or if I was lying.

I took a deep breath and started. I gave her as much detail as I felt was necessary without going overboard. Too much detail usually indicated falsified statements.

"What happened when you got here?" she asked after I'd gone through our entire morning, including the call I received from Patricia saying we had to be at this urgent meeting.

"My mother called when I was in the car, and then we came inside," I said.

"What did she call you for?" Molly asked.

I didn't want to tell her. If I did, it would make me look guilty. Like I had a motive to kill Claudine. "She just wanted to confirm our wedding date."

"Is she making travel arrangements?" Molly asked.

"Yes." I smiled. "When we came inside, Claudine and Roland were in the office with Patricia. Seamus and I sat down, and Patricia told us she'd mistakenly double booked our date."

"Let's head that way, and you can talk me through everything that happened while we retrace your steps," Molly said.

Molly, Seamus, and I started toward Patricia's office in silence.

"Seamus and I were sitting here, and Claudine and Roland were sitting there," I said, pointing to each chair as I said our names. "Patricia was sitting at her desk while her assistant stood off to the side."

"I can imagine it frustrated you when Patricia informed you of her mistake," Molly said.

Seamus squeezed my hand.

"Sure," I said. "I think it would frustrate anyone. Especially when Patricia notified us she had nothing available before August. Though she made it sound like it wasn't her mistake, but her assistant's."

"What happens in August?"

Ugh, why had I said anything about August? "That's when my mom's getting married."

"And what? You want to beat her down the aisle?"

I laughed. That was preposterous. "No, but after her wedding, she's going on a year-long honeymoon and won't be able to attend my wedding until a year from August."

"Right, so you really needed that date, didn't you?"

I knew where she was going with this. "Not enough to kill someone."

"But this is the place where Seamus' entire family has been married, right?"

"That's right," I said, trying to keep my tone neutral through gritted teeth.

"And you probably don't want to wait a year and a half to get married."

"Not particularly."

"Let's keep going. What happened after Patricia told you there weren't any availabilities before August?"

"Claudine and Roland left to figure out some of their plans. And then I went to talk to them one more time." I started out of the room toward the staircase.

"Did you?" Molly asked behind me.

"Did I what?"

"Talk to them?"

I shook my head as I started up the steps. "I heard a couple of people arguing, but I don't know if it was them. I never ended up seeing them. This place is huge. And the next thing I knew, I heard someone scream and a thump. I rushed down to this level from the third, looked over the railing, and saw Claudine lying there." I pointed over the railing where I'd first seen Claudine on the stone floor.

"This is the exact place you looked over?" Molly pointed with her pen at the railing next to me.

"Yes, why?"

"There's blood on the other side of that railing from where I would guess Claudine hit her nose before tumbling to the ground, and there's blood on your pants at approximately the same height," Molly said. "Shayla Murphy, you're under arrest for attempted murder. You are not obliged to say anything unless you wish to do so. Whatever you say will be taken down in writing and may be given in evidence."

4

This couldn't be real. It was just one of those nightmares I'd been having since I started planning the wedding. No way was I being handcuffed by my fiancé's ex. And for murder, nonetheless. It was preposterous. It could only happen in my nightmares, right?

The cuffs felt pretty hard against my wrist bones as Molly clamped them on.

"Yer codding me," Seamus said with a small laugh. "Yer not actually arresting Shayla. That blood probably just transferred from the rails when she looked over."

I glanced down at the tiny stain on my pant leg. If Claudine had broken her nose with that much force, it would have easily left a much bigger stain on my pants had I been standing there when she fell. Or when someone pushed her.

"She's the most likely suspect," Molly said. "I need to talk to her in-depth and process some clues, but yes, I'm arresting her."

Seamus looked shocked but quickly regained his composure as he followed us down the spiral staircase. "Don't say another word, Shay. I'll call the solicitor and have him meet you at the garda station."

Tears stung my eyes as I tried to navigate the steps that had been hard to descend earlier without having my hands tied behind my back. We sounded like a herd of elephants tromping down the stairs—me in the front, Molly behind me, and Seamus right behind her.

We were almost to the bottom when my foot missed a stair, sending me toppling backward onto Molly and sliding down the remaining three stairs on my butt.

I couldn't hold my emotions in any longer.

I burst into sobs.

Everything was going wrong today.

Molly was already back on her feet, and Seamus squeezed past her to help me up. "Come on, love. It's okay. Everything will be just fine."

I looked at the floor where Claudine had been lying.

"When Claudine wakes up, she'll tell you it wasn't me," I said through tears.

"Until that moment, we have to do everything necessary to apprehend who we believe to be the most likely suspect," Molly said as she started pushing me toward the door again.

Seamus was practically pleading with Molly, but she ignored everything he said.

"Thank you for calling us in," Molly said to Patricia. "How many staff members were on the premises today?"

"I can get you a list. But inside were just my two assistants and me," Patricia said.

"And where are they now?" Molly asked.

"Anna is around here somewhere, and I sent Freya home," Patricia said. "She was acting like a blubbering idiot. It didn't reflect properly on the castle."

"Is there any way you can call her and get her to come back?" Molly asked, frustration in her tone.

"I can try her cell," Patricia said. "But I'd like to go to the hospital, if possible, to check on Claudine."

Molly sighed. "Very well. I'll take your statement at the hospital. And if you'd like to ask Freya to head to the hospital instead of back here, that would be incredibly helpful."

"I'll do that," Patricia said, walking ahead of us through the massive wooden door leading outside.

Before we reached the door, another garda rushed to Molly with a phone in his hand. "It's for you."

She stared at him for a moment before taking the phone. "Hello?" Her eyes widened at whatever the person on the other end of the line was saying. "I see." She nodded, her gaze darting to me, then back at the door. "Are you—are you certain? But I have evidence that—" Her body tensed. "I apologize. Yes. Will do."

Molly stared at the phone a moment before handing it back to the man to whom it belonged.

"Is everything okay?" Seamus asked.

She reached down to the cuffs behind my back. I expected her to push me forward again. Instead, she unlocked them.

"You're free to go. For now," Molly said through gritted teeth.

"You mean I'm not under arrest? You don't think I tried to kill Claudine?"

"Oh no," Molly said. "I still think you did. But you're not under arrest. At least, not right now."

I didn't understand. How had everything changed so quickly with one phone call?

"Who was on the phone?" Seamus asked.

"That . . . is none of your business," Molly said. "Before you go, I need to get a few photographs and a swab of the stain on your pants."

It was evident that the blood was Claudine's, but the minuscule amount would hopefully prove that it had been a simple transfer from the balcony spindles.

Once she had all the photographs of my pants, my hands, and a swab sample, she marched back to the crime scene without another word.

"I just need to grab my purse," I said to Seamus as we watched her walk away. "I left it in Patricia's office when I went to talk to Claudine."

Seamus waited at the door while I made my way past the crime scene again, trying to be as invisible as possible so Molly wouldn't yell at me . . . or try to arrest me again.

On the way by, one of the other gardaí showed Molly something on his phone. "She had mascara streaked down her face like she'd been crying. Maybe we should look into the husband."

Molly nodded and continued searching.

The pink of the office seemed so off compared to the situation at hand. I'd always thought of pink as a cheerful color. Not my favorite, but happy.

I reached down to pick up my purse and realized

Patricia had probably left her computer unlocked with all the craziness. I could peek quickly and see if she was telling the truth about not having any dates available.

Had she been lying to me? My gut said yes, but my head said no. Sometimes people just acted icy toward other people. Maybe that was her way of separating her feelings before she had to go into a confrontation, such as telling two brides their wedding date had been double booked.

I glanced out to the main area where Molly and the other gardaí were still working. No one paid me any attention.

I'd just sneak a quick peek.

I slipped behind the desk and crouched down so no one would see over the computer.

When I moved the mouse to activate the monitor, it went to a lock screen.

Dang.

Maybe she had a note with her password or something?

I did a quick once over of her desk, but she seemed to have packed up almost everything that had been there when we met.

It was pointless. There wasn't anything here that would help me.

I groaned in frustration and stood up.

"Find what you were looking for?" Molly stood in the doorway with her hands on her hips.

I stood looking wide-eyed at Molly. She'd caught me red-handed going through Patricia's office. I figured the best thing to do was to come clean. "I wanted to see if she'd been telling the truth about not having any additional availability before August."

"You thought she was lying to you?" Molly's tone was stern, with not a twinge of sympathy.

I shrugged. "I don't know. It was a long shot."

"You're lucky I didn't arrest you. Don't push that luck."

I wanted to come back with something witty about how she'd not chosen to let me out of cuffs, but my words wouldn't form into that perfect witty retort quickly enough.

Instead, I nodded and walked out of the office like a child who had just been reprimanded for stealing a cookie from the cookie jar.

"And leave the investigation up to us," Molly said. "Don't go making a hames of everything because it'll look like you're tampering with an investigation where you're the prime suspect."

As if I'd just leave the investigation up to Molly. She was obviously only seeing one suspect—me. If I wanted to keep myself out of prison, I needed to find out who pushed Claudine off that balcony. And fast.

5

Seamus and I drove almost halfway home in silence. Finally, I got up the nerve to speak. "Are you okay?"

"I'm just processing what happened back there," he said.

I swallowed. "Do you think I did it?"

His head whipped to look at me. "O'course not. I know yeh wouldn't kill anyone. Especially not over a wedding date."

His faith in me was refreshing and nearly always caught me off guard. Growing up, I was always guilty until proven innocent in my mom's eyes.

"Did yeh see anyone up there with her?" Seamus asked.

I shook my head. "By the time I got to the second-floor balcony, whoever pushed her was long gone."

"Does it make me horrible to think we might get our date now?" Seamus asked.

I hadn't even considered that. "No, it doesn't make you horrible. It makes you human."

"A bad human," he said. "I should be worried about Claudine and want her to get better for her wedding, right?"

I shrugged. "We could take her flowers."

"We're already about to take her wedding date. Now you want to take her flowers, too?"

"Not like—" I stopped when I noticed the goofy grin on his face. "Ha. Ha. You know I meant to take flowers to her in the hospital."

"Do yeh think that's a good idea since everyone thinks yeh tried to kill her?" Seamus asked.

"I could wait in the car," I said. "It would be a friendly gesture."

"Maybe tomorrow," Seamus said. "I'm sure she's in surgery now. She won't have a room until the wee hours of the morning, and that's if she makes it through."

"I hope she does," I said. "Then she can tell us who did this."

He grabbed my hand. "When I saw that blonde hair fluttering down, all I could think was that it was you." He cleared his throat of the threatening emotion. "I'm so glad it wasn't."

"I am, too," I said.

"Do you think someone else mixed the two of yeh up?"

"Like someone had been trying to kill me?" I laughed. "Who would want to kill me?"

Seamus didn't answer. His face paled a bit as he focused intently out the front window.

"What are you not telling me?" I asked, dread rising in my stomach.

"I didn't want to worry yeh, but with this, I dunno, I think maybe we should worry."

"What is it?" I asked. "What happened?"

"There's a group—the Anti-Shayla Brigade, or ASB, as they call themselves. We've gotten letters from them."

"Who is we?"

"Me family. Me." Seamus still didn't look over at me. "They started out friendly, saying things like don't marry an American, you're better than that."

"And now?" Dread settled in my chest, making it hard to breathe.

"The most recent one came yesterday," he said. "It was a death threat. I suspect that's the reason Molly took you out of cuffs. When you went up to talk to Claudine, I called me mam and told her about the situation. She was on the phone when I thought I saw you fall. When I picked it back up, I told her you were fine, but another woman had been pushed from the balcony with the same hair."

"You think your mom called the Gardaí and told them about the letters?"

"I'd bet my life on it," Seamus said. "I'm sorry I didn't tell yeh about this before. I didn't think they were impor-tant, and you were already so stressed with the wedding planning and the castle renovations and yer mam. I didn't want to add anything else to yer plate."

"Is that why you've insisted I take a car to town rather than driving myself?"

He finally glanced over at me. "Are you terribly angry?"

Was I? "No," I said. "I wish you would have told me. But I don't think anyone would mistake Claudine for me. She's much thinner than me and has much better style."

Seamus scoffed. "That's not even slightly true. The two of you look very similar."

I glanced down at my muscular thighs and thought about her twiggy legs. "It makes no sense that they'd mistake me for her. I mean, if you're going to push someone over a balcony, wouldn't you wait to make sure the person you're pushing is the right one?"

"Maybe they didn't know there were two curly blonde-headed women in the building," Seamus said.

"So this case could go two different ways," I said. "Which makes it even more challenging to solve."

"Home or dinner out?" Seamus asked.

"Let's go home."

When we walked up the steps to Seamus' parents' house, Gráinne—his mom—burst from the doors and wrapped me in a tight hug. "Are you okay? I'm so sorry they put you in handcuffs. That Molly needs to drop this silly grudge."

"She was just doing her job," I said, shocked that I was defending her. "I was the one looking over the balcony from where the woman who stole my wedding date had fallen."

"Won't you come inside? Magella has cooked up a delicious meal—shepherd's pie."

You'd think I'd have lost my appetite after a day like I had. But the moment she mentioned shepherd's pie, my stomach grumbled.

Magella was a long-time employee but had also been romantically involved with Seamus' Uncle Alabaster. When Alabaster died right before Christmas, he'd left everything except a few odds and ends to Magella and their daughter, Clara.

Gráinne assumed Magella would move away with her newfound wealth, but she surprised all of us by announcing she'd like to stay on in the same role she'd always had. Apparently, she adored working for the O'Malleys.

The cottage where Seamus and I lived had been Alabaster's, but he'd spent most of his time in Magella's staff housing unit with her. It was a wonder no one but Gráinne knew about their multi-decade romance. Especially with the rumor mill as it was in Ballywick.

Though Alabaster had been terribly cranky and Magella was practically a ray of sunshine, so there was that.

"It's good to see you alive," Donal—Seamus' dad—said when we joined him at the large dining room table.

"Why are we eating in here?" Seamus asked. "And why the extra place settings?"

We usually ate in the kitchen at the four-person table since it was typically only Donal, Gráinne, Seamus, and me.

"Shannon, Geoffrey, and Killian have joined us tonight," Gráinne said. "I would guess it's Magella's famous shepherd's pie that lured them out of their caverns."

Magella smiled. "I'd guess they're coming for more than shepherd's pie."

Gráinne laughed. She and Magella had become almost like sisters over the course of the past few months. Magella was helping Gráinne through the loss of a friend, and Gráinne was helping Magella through the loss of her soulmate.

"Speak of the de—" Seamus started, but his father cut him off.

"Shannon, Killian, Geoffrey, it's so good to see you," Donal said, booming with joy.

"Please, come in, sit down," Gráinne said.

"Thank you for having us," Shannon said, then elbowed Geoffrey.

"Yeah, thanks," Geoffrey said.

"Killian," Seamus said, his tone icy.

"Seamus." Killian didn't look up. The last time we'd all sat at this table was for Uncle Alabaster's will reading. Needless to say, it didn't go well for Killian and his parents. By the end, they'd walked away with nothing.

Gráinne and Donal were too kind to let Geoffrey and Shannon live on the streets, though. They'd set them up in one of the empty staff houses, had food delivered to their door weekly, and provided them with a car service to do their business as needed. Geoffrey made some poor business deals in the past but seemed to be making his way back from them.

"Now boys, please try to get along," Gráinne said.

"I agree," Shannon said. "We're family. Let's act like it."

I almost laughed because this was exactly how family acted in my house.

6

"Wait, you're telling me you almost went to jail for offing another bride?" Killian roared with laughter.

Everyone had loosened up with time . . . and alcohol.

"That's exactly what almost happened," I said. "Then Molly gets this phone call, and poof, I'm off the hook."

Everyone turned to look at Gráinne.

"What? I only called to tell them about the threats we'd been getting and how it was slightly suspicious that they had pushed a woman who looked almost identical to Shayla off a balcony."

"I don't think she was identical," I said.

"She was yer doppelgänger," Seamus said.

"Either way," Donal said. "Gráinne did what had to be done. We couldn't let Shayla end up in prison for a murder she didn't commit. And now she has the time to figure out what really happened."

"Safely," Seamus said. "Because someone could still be

out there waiting to kill yeh. Especially when they find out the woman they pushed was Claudine."

"Wait, Claudine with the curly blonde hair?" Killian asked. "She's getting married? To whom?"

"His name is Roland," Seamus said. "I could have guessed yeh'd have known her."

"She went to school with us," Killian said. "Don't yeh remember?"

Seamus shook his head.

"That's because yeh always had yer head in the books. Never wanted to get involved with the ladies," Killian teased. "And look where that got yeh—yer an American park ranger."

"About that," Seamus said. "We're not going back to America. We've decided to stay here."

"Here?" Geoffrey asked. It was the first thing he'd said all night. "Yer staying in Ireland?"

"They are," Gráinne said. "Isn't that exciting?"

"It is exciting, right dear?" Shannon said, her teeth gritted at her husband.

"Grand." Geoffrey's tone said differently.

"Hold on, back up to Claudine," Killian said, and Seamus and I both groaned a bit. "Did yeh say she's with Roland?"

"I think so," Seamus said. "Why?"

"He went to school with us too," Killian said. "He was a right sod, that one. I wouldn't be surprised if he killed her himself. Or had his mummy kill her."

"His mam?" Seamus asked. "Why?"

"Claudine was not in the same league as Roland. If his

family found out she used to be an exotic dancer." Killian ran a finger across his neck.

"Watch what yeh say about the Carraghers," Geoffrey said severely. "The matriarch—Margaret Carragher—is not someone yeh want to cross."

Not a single person at the table disagreed. Not even Gráinne, who knew every person in Ballywick.

"See?" I said. "Maybe those notes were just threats. I'm sure they're nothing to worry about."

"What notes?" Shannon asked.

"Those are the threats we've gotten," Donal said. "At least one every day since they announced their engagement."

I swallowed to keep the shepherd's pie from coming back up. Every day since our engagement? That was a lot of threats.

The entire table stared at me with worried expressions on their faces.

"I'll be careful," I said. "I promise."

This appeased them enough to return their focus to their food.

"I love what yeh've done with the castle," Shannon said. "When it burned down, I didn't think it would ever look the same again."

"Shayla's taken on that project," Seamus said with pride in his voice.

"Well, yeh've done a fantastic job," Shannon said. "Aoife would be thrilled to see it."

No one replied.

Aoife—Killian's sister—had accidentally burned the

castle down. And purposely killed Uncle Alabaster. She wasn't the most popular topic in the house.

"How is Aoife?" Gráinne said, her voice tight like the words had barely squeaked out. "Have yeh visited much?"

"We've been a time or two," Shannon said, not looking at either her son or husband. "Well, I have."

"There's no reason for me to visit," Geoffrey said. "Not after she sent me that nasty letter."

"She was just upset," Shannon whispered. "Yer her father. Yeh need to be the bigger person."

Geoffrey's face turned red, but he said nothing else.

"And what about you, Killian? Haven't been to see yer sister?" Seamus asked. He was probably the only person who could get away with questioning Killian like that.

"No time," Killian said flippantly. "I've been delightfully busy with the new position and everything."

"I'm so glad that's working out for yeh," Gráinne said. She'd set him up with a job in Dublin doing office financial work. "Do tell the ladies in the office hello for me."

Killian grinned. I suspected he'd familiarized himself well with the ladies in the office.

"Wow, look how late it's gotten," Donal said. "We best be getting ready for bed."

Shannon, Geoffrey, and Killian took their cue that it was time to go.

"Please come back for dinner again sometime," Gráinne said. "It was lovely to have the family back together."

Geoffrey didn't reply.

Shannon nodded. "I think we'd like that. And thank

yeh so much for all yeh've done to help us get back on our feet. We appreciate it more than we can say."

"Family helps family," Gráinne said. "No matter the circumstance."

I stood as well. "Killian, do you think I could have a moment before you go?"

Seamus eyed me suspiciously.

"I just want to ask you a bit more about Claudine and Roland."

Killian looked at his watch, then looked up at me and smirked. "'Course I have time for yeh. Seamus, pour us another round, will yeh?"

As Killian and I made our way to the sitting room, Seamus dutifully did as he was told with a mock salute.

"What is it yeh want to know?" Killian asked.

"How did you know Claudine was an exotic dancer?" I asked.

Killian didn't blush or look even slightly taken aback by my question. "I saw her, o'course. She was working at one of the higher-class joints in Dublin. I'd suspect that's where she and Roland reconnected."

"Roland went to these clubs?" I asked.

"Went?" Killian laughed. "He still goes. I saw him there just the other night."

"What night?" I asked.

Seamus handed Killian a drink and sat beside me on the comfy sofa.

"I suppose it was two nights ago," Killian said. "Or maybe last night? I can't be certain, me days and nights run together."

"Did you ever date Claudine?" I asked.

"Date would be a strong word," Killian said. "We had some fun together once or twice, but I don't date strippers. Unlike Roland, I have standards."

I didn't mention how the last woman he'd dated had obviously only been with him for his money. When she realized he didn't have any, she bolted.

"How long ago did you *have fun*?" I asked.

"No, no, no," Killian said. "Don't put that on me. There was no ring on her spectacularly adept hand when I was with her. Explains why she's not dancing at the club anymore."

"Does Roland still go?"

Killian shrugged. "Roland did what Roland wanted. Claudine had to have known that before she accepted his proposal."

"What could have happened if she hadn't gone along with Roland's wishes?"

"He never grew out of the temper tantrum phase. Though, the bigger he got, the bigger his tantrums got."

A weight settled in my stomach.

I needed to talk to Roland.

7

Seamus held the biggest bouquet of flowers we could find in Ballywick as he walked into the hospital to deliver them to Claudine. He'd specifically instructed me to stay in the car.

I hadn't agreed, which only made him laugh. I couldn't imagine being with a man who only cared about himself. A man like Roland.

It didn't matter that he was wealthy and she was an exotic dancer. If they were engaged, he should treat her with respect.

Rain misted the windshield, making the entire world look blurry. I closed my eyes and tried to picture everything that had happened at the Ballywick Castle the day before.

I'd been upstairs—on the third level—when I heard Claudine say, "Ouch."

Had someone grabbed her? Maybe she was looking over the balcony, upset from an argument with Roland, and someone grabbed her hair.

Then she said, "What are you talking about?" At least, I thought that was what she had been about to say until her voice turned into a scream of terror.

Maybe Roland accused her of going back to the club. Or cheating on him.

A tap on the glass made me nearly hit my head on the car's roof.

I couldn't determine who was on the other side of the glass. If only I could wipe the condensation away.

The person did it for me, then cupped their hands and peered into the window, their gaze locking with mine, scaring them enough to make them jump backward.

I laughed aloud.

It was Molly, and she'd nearly fallen on her butt.

I turned the key in the ignition and rolled the window down enough to see her. "You okay?"

She glared at me. "Oh, don't tell me yeh weren't just in there laughing."

"Hey, you scared me too."

She brushed off her backside that had contacted the car next to ours. "What are yeh doing here?"

"Seamus is just taking Claudine some flowers," I said. "It's nothing to worry about."

"Sure," she said. "I've learned when it comes to you, there's always something to worry about."

"What do you mean by that? If I remember correctly, I'm the one who saved your butt in that castle, and I'm the one who solved the last murder."

"Exactly my point. Yer always right in the thick of things. And now I find yeh here. Stalking a woman yeh tried to kill once already."

I gritted my teeth. "I did not try to kill her."

"Then why the flowers?" Molly asked. "Feeling guilty, are yeh? Or maybe yeh came to make sure they were changing their wedding date."

My heart raced. Was she saying they'd changed it or was that just a guess?

"Neither," I said. "I'm here because we wanted to bring Claudine flowers."

"And?"

"And nothing." I wasn't about to tell her it would have been a lucky coincidence if I ran into Roland in the parking lot.

"Stay out of my way in this case," Molly said, her tone harsh. "You do not want to get on my bad side."

I put on my cop voice. "I thought I was already on your bad side, seeing as how I'm getting ready to marry your ex."

"I left him," she said. "I don't give a—"

"Everything okay in here?" Seamus said as he opened the driver's side door.

"Grand," Molly said. "I'm watching the both of yeh."

"Feel free," I said. "I'll be waiting for your call."

"My call? Why would I call you?"

"Two reasons—one for help on the case."

Molly scoffed.

"And two, to apologize."

"I wouldn't hold yer breath."

I sucked in a breath and puffed out my cheeks.

"That's something my daughter—a child—would do. Don't act like a child." Molly stormed away, not glancing back at us once.

"How'd it go in there?" I asked Seamus after letting the air out of my lungs and cheeks.

"Better than in here," he said. "Which isn't saying much."

"At least they took the flowers," I said, noting he didn't have them in his hands any longer.

"Oh, sure. Roland took 'em all right. Took 'em and chucked 'em in the bin."

I winced.

"But on the bright side, we have our wedding date back." Seamus smiled. "I even called to confirm it with Patricia."

"Did you ask about the wedding date before or after he chucked the flowers in the trash?"

"After," Seamus said. "Though, now I'm thinking I should have asked before. Then I could have gifted the rejected flowers to another patient."

"How is Claudine?"

"She's stable but unconscious," Seamus said. "They don't know if she has permanent brain damage."

"That's horrible," I said. "But at least she's alive."

"At least she's alive," Seamus agreed.

"I'm guessing you didn't get any information from Roland about the club, then?"

"Not a bit. He wasn't exactly in the mood to speak to me."

"How will we get him to talk?"

"Maybe Killian will help," Seamus said. "For the right price, I'm sure he'll be up for it."

"You think we'll have to pay him?"

"This is the same lad who used to force me to pay him

every time he got my lunch back from bullies." Seamus laughed. "He does nothing for free."

"I suppose it would be worth it if we could get information from Roland."

"Let's ring him, shall we?"

"Sure, I'll do it," Killian said.

"How much?" Seamus asked, holding the phone on speaker while we sat in the hospital parking lot.

"I'm not gonna charge yeh." Killian laughed.

Seamus looked at me, then back at the phone with suspicion written all over his face. "Yer not?"

"Yeh sound surprised, cousin."

"Won't lie, I am."

"Can't family do things to help one another? Like yer mam was saying last night?"

Seamus looked at me. I shrugged.

"I suppose so," Seamus finally said. "Erm, thanks. When do yeh think is best?"

"Tonight," Killian said. "He'll be at the club."

"With his fiancée in the hospital?" I asked.

"His favorite dancer will be there," Killian said. "He won't be missing it."

"Great, then tonight it is," Seamus said.

"I will need a few things to make it successful."

Seamus glanced up at me with a justified look on his face. "What yeh be needing?"

"A new suit, for one," Killian said. "All mine are at the cleaners. Plus, the cover charge, drink costs, and money for the girls."

"Anything else?" Seamus said with a smile and a shake of his head.

"I'll think about it," Killian said. "Pick me up at six."

"We'll ring yeh when we get there." Seamus hung up the phone. "Looks like we're going to Dublin."

I'd only been to Dublin once when I flew into the airport. Since Christmas and the proposal, I'd been busy settling into the cottage and working on the castle restoration. We would have plenty of time to travel and see the country after the wedding.

The rain fell harder as we got onto the interstate-like road. I was still getting used to being on the left side of the road with the fast lane on the right. I'd driven around Ballywick but hadn't ventured onto the quicker roads.

"Will we have him record the conversation?" I asked. "Or just rely on his recounting of the story? Because if he's drinking, we may not get the entire story—not that he'd lie—but he might forget."

Seamus laughed. "We'll listen in. I have a contact in the city who can provide us with all the equipment the Gardaí use."

"Oh good, that'll be good." Excitement and worry flowed through me in equal parts.

Seamus reached over and grabbed my hand in his. "It'll be fine. Try to stop worryin' so much."

"Sorry," I said.

"And no more apologizing either," Seamus said. "What am I gonna do with yeh?"

"Marry me and give me lots of babies?" I said, without thinking.

"How many is lots?" Seamus asked.

We hadn't had this conversation. Sure, we both wanted kids, but he didn't know my outrageous fantasy of having a whole houseful of kids.

"I don't know," I said. "How many do you think?"

"Never really thought about it," Seamus said. "'Course I want kids. Just don't know how many. I'm fine with whatever."

"Whatever?" I raised my eyebrows.

"Lay it on me, love. What's yer thoughts?"

"Eight." I let the word slip out before I could overthink it.

Seamus stared out the windshield, his face unchanged. Maybe he hadn't heard me.

I was about to repeat it when he turned to look at me. "Let's make it nine, and we can have our own football team."

"Don't joke," I said. "I'm serious."

"So am I," Seamus said. "But I get to be the goalkeeper."

"I guess I'll have to learn to play soccer—I mean —football."

Seamus beamed at me. How had I gotten so lucky?

Dublin was even better than I'd imagined. Colorful doors brightened the dreary day as we drove through neighborhoods and past ultra-green parks.

"Where are we going?" I asked. "I figured we'd head into the city."

"We're meeting Killian at his flat and then taking him to get his new suit," Seamus said. "While he's getting fitted, we'll pick up the tech stuff."

Killian stood outside his building holding an umbrella, waiting for us. When we pulled up to the curb, he jumped into the back seat, shaking his umbrella. Too bad most of the rainwater landed on me instead of outside the car.

"Sorry we can't go up," Killian said. "The roommate has a girl over."

I suspected it was more than that. By the looks of the place, this was not the type of residence to which Killian was accustomed.

"It's no bother," Seamus said. "Maybe another time. Shall we be on with the suit shopping?"

"We shall," Killian said. "Is there anything specific you want me to ask Roland? Do you want me to come out and ask if he tried to kill his fiancée?"

"No," I said, turning to look at him in the back seat. "That would be a horrible idea."

Killian patted me on the shoulder. "I'm just codding yeh. I know a thing or two about interrogation tactics."

"This is not an interrogation," I said. "We just want to know if their relationship was solid. And why might he have been arguing with her right before she fell?"

"And if there's anyone else who might have wanted her dead," Seamus added.

"What if he doesn't want to talk about it?" Killian asked.

"Give him more alcohol," I said. "Spare no expense. Make him think you're his best friend in the entire world. You were popular in school, right?"

"Well . . ."

"He was popular," Seamus said. "No need to act modest when you're the furthest thing from it."

"All right, I was popular."

"And Roland was not, I assume?" I asked.

"Not in the least," Seamus said.

"Then he'll likely want to do anything he can to get in your good graces," I said.

"He does like to follow me around like a puppy when we're at the club." Killian let out a sound of disgust.

"Use that to your advantage," I said. "He'll be eager to please you. And will likely want to tell you about his issues. You could act like you don't even know what happened with Claudine at first."

"Ooh, that's good," Killian said. "Then he won't think I'm in cahoots with the two of yeh."

"And it'll be good to hear it from his perspective," Seamus said. "Maybe he'll give away more than he realizes."

I smiled.

This was going to work.

8

Killian walked into the fancy-looking clothing store with Seamus' platinum card and a smile.

"Are you sure you trust him with that?" I asked.

"Not in the slightest," Seamus said but left it at that.

We drove into a sketchy area and down an alley before Seamus pulled the car to the side, and we came to a stop. "Don't worry. It's not as scary as it looks."

"I was a police officer, remember? Not a lot scares me." I smirked.

Seamus leaned over and kissed me on the cheek. "Forgive me. I know yer a baddie."

"A baddie?" I laughed.

"Ah yeh know what I mean." He smiled. "Get out of the car so we can get this done."

He knocked on a metal door next to a gray dumpster.

A woman opened the door wearing a tight red dress, matching lipstick, and long dark hair. "What's the craic?"

"Divil a bit," Seamus said. "Good seeing yeh, Randy. How are things?"

Randy eyed me over Seamus' shoulder. "Things are much sadder without you around." She ran a hand down his arm.

He chuckled nervously and took a step back. "This is me fiancée, Shayla. Shayla, this is Randy. We used to date."

Seamus was becoming famous in my book for keeping tidbits like this to himself and springing them on me at the last moment. Like the fact that he was a gazillionaire.

"It's a pleasure to meet you, Randy." I held out a hand to shake hers, but she ignored me and turned back to Seamus.

"We did more than just date," she said with a wink.

I did my best to keep my expression neutral. I wouldn't give her the satisfaction of knowing how hurt I was that Seamus hadn't told me all of this himself. "I'm sure you had some great times together."

She looked at me as if I wasn't allowed to speak.

"Right," Seamus said, rocking back on his heels. "Is Ilona around?"

"She's getting everything together for yeh," Randy said. "I was just heading out, but I couldn't leave before I got to see yeh."

"That was nice of you to stay. Do tell your brother hello for me."

"You should do that yourself. He'd love to hear from yeh."

I wanted to sink into a hole. Or run back to the car. Or perhaps run back to the car and drive it into a sinkhole.

Randy pulled on a cropped leather jacket with a button on the front. *Say No to Shayla* was in bright red letters with a red circle around a picture of my face and a matching line slashing through it.

"What is that?" Seamus asked. "Don't tell me yer one of them."

She shrugged. "Some of us think yeh should try to find a good Irish girl."

"Some of you would be wrong." Seamus seemed just as mad as I was. "Who is in charge of this little club? I need to have words with them."

"No one knows how it started." Randy took a step toward Seamus. "But even if I did know, I wouldn't tell you." She grabbed his chin and planted a big red kiss on his lips.

Before he could pull away, she walked away down the alley toward the main road.

"I'm sorry about her." A tiny mouse-like woman appeared inside the door with large glasses and a head of messy brown hair. "She is such a hussy." She hurried to the doorway. "Come in, come in. You must be Shayla. It's wonderful to meet yeh."

We followed her inside. My heart was racing uncontrollably. How dare Randy kiss Seamus in front of me like that? How dare she kiss him at all?

"I presume yer not part of that stupid club," Seamus asked.

"Randy tries to get me to join all the time, but it's ridiculous. Yeh should be able to marry whomever yeh want just like the rest of us."

"Much appreciated," Seamus said. "Now, if we could

just get them to stop sending hate mail, that would be wonderful."

Ilona frowned and pushed her glasses up her nose, making her eyes look huge. "Hate mail? I didn't know they were sending hate mail. Randy goes on and on about how they're peacefully protesting."

"The Gardaí are monitoring it," Seamus said with a shrug. "Now, were yeh able to get all the items?"

"And then some." Ilona's face lit up. "It's all state-of-the-art. You could be miles away and still hear everything like yeh were sitting right next to them." She handed Seamus a box full of equipment. "This will record the conversation. These are the batteries. Change them before they completely run out of juice."

"Savage," Seamus said, pulling out a check and handing it to her. "Yer the best."

She opened it, and her eyes widened. "I could say the same about you."

Seamus slipped the box into the back seat while I let myself in the passenger door.

"We just need to pick up Killian and make sure he's ready," Seamus said, turning the car on and starting down the alley.

"You're kidding, right?" I asked, trying to keep myself from blowing up.

"Er—no," Seamus said. "Don't tell me yeh changed yer mind. I just spent a small fortune back there, and I doubt she'd be keen on returns."

"I'm not talking about the equipment or the plan," I said. "I'm talking about yet another surprise in the form of an evil brown-haired kissing monster."

Seamus glanced over at me and then burst into laughter.

Usually, I would have laughed with him. I mean, it was a funny description. But I wasn't in the mood to laugh. "I'm being serious. I am sick of being blindsided by your secrets everywhere I turn."

"Do yeh want me to tell yeh about every girl I ever dated?" Seamus asked. "I will. But they mean nothing to me now. Plus, I had no idea Randy would be there. She and Ilona never seemed to like each other much."

Tears stung my eyes.

Seamus reached up and brushed my hair out of my face. "I love you, Shayla. No one else. I have a past full of things I would never regret because they led me to you. But that's where those things and people will stay—in the past."

He was right. He couldn't possibly tell me everything about his life. And living in Ireland, we would run into people from his past. "I'm sorry. I didn't mean to get so upset."

"It's no bother," he said. "Get upset with me anytime yeh want. Just as long as yeh end up back in my arms."

When we arrived at the shop to pick up Killian, we had returned to our smiley selves.

9

Seamus and I huddled in the car listening to Killian as he made his way through the club, greeting every person—primarily women—by name.

"He's smooth," I said.

"Too smooth sometimes." Seamus checked the battery on the recording device for the tenth time in as many minutes. "This equipment is amazing."

"Ilona was right," I said. "It does sound like we're right there with him."

"Which could get interesting by the end of the night."

I laughed. "I'm ready if you are."

"There's the man of the hour," Killian said, making my ears perk up. "Roland, my man. What's the craic?"

Roland's response was drowned out by what sounded like a bro hug, complete with loud pats on the back.

"How's the missus?" Killian asked.

I cringed. "He's going in too soon."

Seamus winced.

"She's doing great," Roland said. "Planning our wedding as we speak."

"And where does she think you are at this time of night?" Killian asked, not missing a beat over the overt lie.

"Work in the city," Roland said. "Let's face it. If she wants pretty things, I need to work."

"Do yeh though?" Killian asked, a twinge of jealousy in his voice.

"With me mam breathing down me neck, I do." Roland's voice got so quiet I almost couldn't hear. "This round's on me." He had to have been speaking to a waitress. Several people around cheered for the free round.

"What's yer mam on about this time?" Killian asked. How he conversed with Roland was almost as if they were friends.

"She's hired someone to follow Claudine around to prove to me I should marry someone else—someone more proper. Little does she know, I met Claudine here." Roland laughed. "Those were the good old days."

"Come on now, the good old days don't have to end, do they? Just because yer getting hitched?" Killian asked.

"Can I tell yeh something I haven't told anyone here?" Roland whispered. He had to have leaned into Killian right where the mic was for us to hear it over the club's noise.

"I'm all ears," Killian said.

I held my breath. Was he about to confess everything? Or even just tell the truth about Claudine lying in a hospital bed?

"I truly love her," Roland said. "I know I'm here

several nights a week, but it's only to keep up appearances. She's the love of my life."

"Keep up appearances for who?" Killian asked. "If yeh love her, shouldn't yeh be with her?"

I gasped. He couldn't tell Roland he knew Claudine was in the hospital.

"Me da is right over there," Roland said. "He's keeping an eye on me. While me mam wants me to find someone right for me—someone who will keep me out of the clubs —me da wants to make sure I'm not so love-struck I can't do the job."

"Working for family is rubbish," Killian said. "Strike out on yer own. You can do it."

"Oh, like you?" Roland joked. "You can barely afford the bu—"

"Why didn't you tell me Claudine was in the hospital?" Killian blurted out.

I nearly came out of my seat. What was he doing?

Roland hissed, "Keep yer voice down. I have clients here."

"Well? Why?"

"How did yeh know about Claudine?"

"Did yeh push her, Roland?" Killian asked. "Or did yer mam do it?"

Shoot.

He was taking all the questions we'd given him—the ones to ask when Roland was drunk—and spraying them at Roland like a machine gun.

"I would never," Roland said. "I just told yeh, I love Claudine more than anything in this world."

"Not more than yer job," Killian said. "She's in the

hospital and yer here at a strip club. Yeh should be ashamed."

"Who asked you?" Roland asked. "You're nothing but a broke, unemployed, wannabe businessman."

Killian sputtered, "I—you—that's not—yeh don't know what yer talking about."

"I know yer auntie had to bribe someone to get you a job because no one wanted to hire the murderer's brother. And yeh couldn't even keep it. I know yeh live in a rubbish flat with two guys to a room. I know Nuala left you because yeh gave all yer money away in the heat of the moment."

The next thing we heard was a crunching sound, then gasps followed by muffled grunts and the scuffling of feet. They were physically fighting right there in the middle of the club.

"All right, that's enough," a booming voice said. "Out with you both. And don't come back."

Seamus and I turned to see the club door open, and a bouncer throw Killian and Roland out onto the sidewalk.

"Now look what yeh did, me da's gonna be right furious," Roland said.

"I suppose now you can go be with the woman you say you love," Killian said. "Unless you tried to murder her."

We watched as Roland pulled his fist back and swung at Killian. Roland may have been wealthier, but Killian was quicker. He darted out of the way of Roland's fist, sending Roland spinning and falling onto the concrete.

"That was pathetic," Killian said. "Come on, get up and hit me. Just like you hit Claudine."

"I'd never hit Claudine," Roland shouted.

"But you were arguing before she fell, weren't yeh?"

Roland got to his feet, and the two men squared up as if they were in the boxing ring. People on the sidewalk started to stop and stare.

"Why would you think we were arguing?"

"Couples argue a lot around wedding time. At least that's what I'm told," Killian said. "Maybe she realized she could find someone with half yer money but twice yer looks."

Roland threw another punch, this time landing on Killian's shoulder.

Killian laughed. "That was better."

"Couples argue," Roland said between his heavy breathing. "Claudine loved—loves—me."

"Then why did yeh push her?"

"I didn't push her," Roland said. This time, his punch hit the mark.

Killian went down, his knees buckling, and his limbs going limp.

"That's just grand," Seamus said, pulling his earpiece out and bursting from the car.

I did the same and hurried to follow Seamus across the street to check on Killian.

"Did I kill him?" Roland asked. "I didn't know I could punch so hard."

Seamus checked Killian. "Yeh just knocked him out. He's still breathing."

Roland interlaced his fingers and reached his hands to the top of his head, taking deep breaths as if he'd just run a marathon. When his gaze landed on me, his eyes narrowed. "What are you doing here?"

10

Roland stared at me. "I should have known not to trust him. He would never have taken my side over his precious cousin's."

"What happened before she went over the edge?" I asked. "I heard you arguing. What were you arguing about?"

"You don't know what you heard," Roland said, dropping his arms to his sides. "We were perfectly happy that we'd gotten our date. We were planning the wedding. Everything was going to be perfect. Until you threw her over the balcony in a jealous rage."

Roland was in my face now, but I wasn't about to back down.

"I didn't push her," I said. "You did."

"That's ridiculous. Why would I push her?"

"Maybe she found out you were still coming to the club, and she threatened to leave you if you didn't stop." I shrugged. "Or maybe she said she didn't want to marry you anymore because your mom was stalking her."

Roland clenched his fists. Something I'd said had struck a nerve.

"I'll ask you one more time. What were you arguing about?" I asked. "I heard you. She was upset. Why was she upset?"

"Fine. Yer right. She found out I was still coming to the club," Roland said, then exhaled as if a load had been taken off his shoulders. "I told her it meant nothing. That I was just doing it to appease me da, but she didn't believe me. She was going to leave me. But I didn't push her. I wanted to win her back, not kill her."

"What happened after you argued?" I asked.

"She left me on the third floor," Roland said. "I wanted to go after her, but she told me not to. If only I had, maybe this would have been prevented. I could have stopped whoever did this."

"And where did you go?"

"I waited a while, then went back downstairs too. That's when I heard a scream. My entire world fell apart when I saw Seamus move her hair and realize she wasn't you."

"But she's alive," I said. "And you're not at the hospital. What if she wakes up and finds out you were at the strip club while she was in a hospital bed? I'd guess she wouldn't be very keen on taking you back."

"The doctors said she wouldn't wake up any time soon," Roland said. "I've had this scheduled for months. I was meeting a big client here. Which won't be happenin' now, thanks to Killian."

"If you didn't push her over that railing," I asked. "Who do you think did?"

He stared down at the ground and shook his head.

I gave him a couple of long minutes before I asked again, "Who would have wanted Claudine dead?"

His voice came back almost inaudibly, "Me mam."

<hr>

Roland returned to the club with a fair bit of cash and his father's assistance.

Meanwhile, Killian had regained consciousness and was annoying Seamus and me with all the details of what had happened over and over again.

"I think he has a concussion," I whispered to Seamus as Killian started his story over for the umpteenth time. "We can't leave him at his apartment alone."

"I think he has roommates," Seamus said.

"But what if they don't take care of him? He could fall asleep and never wake up."

"Killian," Seamus interrupted Killian mid-sentence. "How about we take you to yer mam and da's tonight so they can keep an eye on yeh 'till morning?"

"No way," Killian said. "I want nothing to do with those gombeens. Take me to me flat. I'll be fine."

"If we take you to your flat, we're coming up with you and making sure someone's there to watch you through the night," I said. "Which means we'll see where you live."

"Ah, right," Killian said. "Don't want that. Then you'll know how much I'm struggling. But I can't go to me mam's."

"Let's take him to the cottage," I said. "But first, we need to take him to the hospital."

Seamus nodded.

Killian objected.

I sighed.

It was going to be a long night.

The doctor confirmed that Killian had a severe concussion and recommended he stay in the hospital overnight. Seamus and I promised to come back the next day to check on him and take him back to his flat.

We would have stayed with him, but I had an early morning meeting with one of the contractors for the castle, and Seamus needed to check on the horses.

"Do yeh think he'll be okay?" Seamus asked as we made our way back across the country.

"I'm sure he'll be fine," I said. "But it's good we took him to the hospital. I feel terrible that we put him in that position."

"Killian's the one who put himself in that position," Seamus said. "He's been known to get into some tight spots. What do yeh think about Roland?"

"I don't know," I said. "On one hand, he seems to care about Claudine. But on the other, why isn't he at her bedside? Is business so much more important than being with the one you love?"

"To some, yes," Seamus said, pulling my hand up to his lips and kissing my palm. "But not to everyone. I'm sure Claudine knew what she was getting herself into when she started dating him."

"But she was going to leave him because he was going to the club," I said.

"Or so he says," Seamus said. "Maybe it was more than that. Who knows?"

"He threw his mom under the bus pretty readily."

"From the sound of things, she's not a very nice person."

"I need to talk to her. If she were at Ballywick Castle that day, she'd definitely be a suspect." Molly had probably already talked to her, so I'd have to get creative to find out where she'd been that day.

"We can worry about all that tomorrow," Seamus said.

I closed my eyes and laid my head against the cool window. Tomorrow was another day.

11

The next morning, I woke before the sun rose to get a head start on the castle restoration. The contractors arrived early most days, and I didn't want to make them wait.

"Hello there, Cupid," I said as I walked the fence line between the cottage and the castle. Cupid—my favorite horse on the farm—trotted next to me with his cute fuzzy face and heart-shaped marking on his face. "How are you today?"

He threw his head back and let out an enthusiastic whinny.

"That good, huh?"

He got close enough to the fence to reach over and grab the sleeve of my jacket, stopping me in my tracks.

"Just a few pats, then I have to go to work."

I'd met Cupid when he was only just born. He and I had grown quite fond of one another since. He often woke me with his whinnies and grunts if I slept too late.

He laid his head against my chest. I wrapped my arms

around his neck and kissed him between his ears. "Okay, buddy. I have to go. I'll be back in a little bit."

Cupid followed me as long as he could and then waited with big brown eyes at the corner of the fence, watching as I walked away.

"Oh, come on, don't give me that look," I said. I ran back to the fence for one more hug. "That's the last one. I'll be back."

He reared back and started bucking and kicking like a toddler who had just gotten their way.

"Yeah, yeah," I said. "You win."

The contractors were only slightly behind schedule. They had added mortar to the castle's stone walls where it had broken down in the fire.

"It's looking fantastic," I said to the head contractor —Milton.

"I'm glad yeh think so." Milton handed me a hard hat. He always wore the same thing—a long-sleeved gray shirt, blue jeans, and a yellow vest. With his graying beard, clean clothes, and crinkles around his eyes, he was obviously the boss. "We're tuckpointing today."

"Great," I said. I had no idea what tuckpointing was, but that's why I'd hired Milton. "Is there anything you need from me?"

"Not right now. I'll need yeh to finalize some of the interior plans when we get there, but for now, we're all set."

"Thank you for everything you do, Milton. I don't know what I'd do without you."

"Don't get all mushy on me," Milton said, but I could

see the blush forming beneath his hairy face. "Before yeh go, what happened the other day with that girl?"

This stopped me in my tracks. "What do you mean, what happened?"

"Rumor is, yeh pushed her right off the roof." He glanced back at a couple of his workers gathering items from the pickup.

"I see," I said, following his gaze. "What else have you heard?"

"Just that yeh were mad that she took yer wedding date, so you tried to kill her." He took a slight step to the left, blocking my view of the men.

"Do you mind telling me who told you this?" I tried to see around him, but every time I moved, he did too.

"That won't help yeh. They probably heard it from someone who heard it from someone else. You know how it works around here."

That I did.

"If you hear anything else, let me know. Thanks again." I handed him the hard hat and took a large step in the other direction. When my gaze landed on the men, I realized what he was trying to hide. They wore the same Anti-Shayla buttons Randy had been wearing the night before.

My breath caught in my chest, and I turned to leave. I didn't have the energy to deal with this. Not from my own crew.

"But wait," Milton said from behind me. "Did yeh do it?"

I turned to look at him. "Milton, do you think I did it?"

"Well, no, but it seems the women in this family are more than they appear."

"I'm not technically in this family yet," I said. "And no, I didn't push or try to kill her."

"Good to hear," Milton said.

"I'd appreciate it if you'd give your crew the memo for me."

He nodded—an understanding passing between us.

I walked away as quickly as possible. Tears stung my eyes. When I reached the corner of the fence line, Cupid stood waiting. I pulled his head into my chest and cried into his mane.

"What wrong, love?"

I hadn't realized Seamus was standing right around the corner. I brushed the tears from my face, but it was too late. He'd already seen me.

"Why are yeh crying?"

"It's nothing," I said. "How are the horses?"

"Is everything okay with the build? Did Milton say something stupid?"

"It's fine," I said. "Everything's fine."

Seamus softened. "It's not fine. Please tell me what's the matter."

"Some of the crew were wearing those Anti-Shayla pins," I said. "It's no big deal. It's not like there's anything we can—"

"Oh, something will be done all right." Seamus stormed away.

I followed behind, trying to get him to stop. I hated creating a fuss. They had a right to their opinions. Not everyone had to like me.

"Milton, a word?" Seamus said, his voice tense but quiet.

Milton walked toward us with a nervous look on his face. "I know what this is about. I tried to get them to take the pins off, but—"

"I'll give yeh an hour to get rid of the pins or the workers wearing them. If I see one more piece of Anti-Shayla propaganda on this property that can be traced back to your men, I'll fire yer entire company on the spot."

I'd never seen such a protective side of Seamus. It made me equal parts happy and mortified.

"I'll have to fire half of me crew," Milton said. "It's a peaceful organization. They're just wearing their beliefs on their shirts."

"The ASB is not a peaceful organization. It's yer choice what to do," Seamus said. "Pack up and leave if yeh prefer. But no one associated with an organization threatening my fiancée will work on my property."

"Threatens?" Milton's eyes went wide. "I'm so sorry, Shayla. I didn't know. I'll get on it right away."

I nodded.

Seamus grabbed my hand—his clammy and shaking—and led me away from Milton.

When I looked back, I saw Milton approach the two men and order them off the job.

12

Seamus and I walked back to the house with Cupid trotting next to us, probably confused as to why we weren't chatting.

When we walked into his parents' house, Gráinne greeted us with a massive smile. "Just in time for breakfast." Her smile faded when she saw the looks on our faces. "What happened to the two of yeh?"

"Some of Milton's men were wearing Anti-Shayla buttons," Seamus said. "I told him to get them off the property, or I'd be firing his entire company."

"I'm sorry. What were they wearing now?" Gráinne growled.

"They're just these stupid buttons," I said. "They have my face and a circle with a slash through them."

"And he let them wear those here? While working for yeh?" Gráinne was a mama bear ready to defend her young.

"It's taken care of for now," Seamus said. "He's the best in the business."

"I don't care if he's the best in the world. He should have fired them the moment they arrived wearing the buttons." Gráinne started toward the door.

"Mam, stop," Seamus said. "He didn't seem to know the group had been sending us threatening letters—said they were a peaceful group. He just thought they were expressing their beliefs—regardless of how stupid those beliefs may be. Give him a chance to make it right. If he doesn't, I'll let yeh do the honors."

Gráinne huffed, then moved to my side and wrapped an arm around my shoulders. "I'm so sorry yeh have to go through all this."

The tears that sprung to my eyes weren't those of anger or hurt anymore. They were the tears of a little girl who didn't have a supportive mother growing up. Sometimes I had to pinch myself to make sure I wasn't dreaming. Not that my mother could help it—she just wasn't wired the same way as Gráinne.

"It'll all be okay," I said. "We'll get married in June, and they'll have to give up, right?"

Their mutual hesitation made my stomach churn.

I glanced down at the food in front of me. There was no way I'd be able to eat without making myself sick. My nerves were getting the better of me.

"I think we'll skip breakfast," Seamus said as if reading my mind. "But thank Magella for us. I'm sure it'll be just as good heated up tomorrow."

"I'd offer it to Milton's crew, but after all this, he won't be seeing one more crumb from my kitchen." Gráinne took a piece of black pudding and shoved it into her mouth before walking out of the room.

"Thank you," I said to Seamus.

"It's no bother. You never have to eat breakfast if yeh don't want to."

"Not for breakfast," I said. "For standing up for me with Milton."

"And you were trying to stop me." Seamus grinned.

"I knew it would be awkward."

"I'd get all kinds of awkward for yeh."

I laughed. "What an interesting thing to say. But I appreciate it."

"Do yeh still feel up to talking to Roland's mam?" He rubbed my lower back. "Because we can always just leave it up to Molly."

"I'm up for it," I said. "I'll get my emotions together on the ride over."

Gráinne had given us the insider scoop about where Margaret hung out every Thursday. I gaped at the extravagance when we pulled up the drive to the day spa.

Nestled in the green hills amongst large trees was a glass structure, though you couldn't see in from the outside. Instead, it reflected its surroundings like one big mirror.

"How do they keep it from reflecting the sun and burning holes in everything?" I asked.

"That's a good question," Seamus said. "I've never thought about it."

"From your mom's intel, Margaret should be heading to lunch now."

"I'll get yeh in, but then yer on yer own. She'll recognize me."

The plan was that I'd pretend to be one of Patricia's

assistants since I knew the most about Patricia and the venue. My tactic was to inform her that a date had opened up and they could get it if they'd jump on it immediately.

Hopefully, she'd tell me how much she hates Claudine and then confess to pushing her over the balcony.

I laughed to myself. If only it were that easy.

Seamus got me into the spa with no issues. The woman at the desk seemed happy to help me with whatever I needed. He gave me a thumbs up as I walked toward the dining room.

There were only two occupied tables—one with a group of women my age, the other with an older woman I assumed was Margaret.

I put on my fake smile and hurried over to her table. "Mrs. Carragher?"

She placed the book she'd been reading on the table with the cover of the naked man chest facing upward with no sense of shame. "Who's asking?"

"I'm Gabby," I said. "I work for Patricia at the Bally-wick Castle. I'm sorry to bother you here, but I couldn't reach you on your cell."

"Cell service is nonexistent up here. It's part of the charm." She looked me up and down. "I wasn't aware Patricia had an American working for her."

Crap. I hadn't even considered attempting an Irish accent.

"I'm new," I said.

"Get on with it. What caused you to come all the way out here and harass me on my single day of peace?"

"Yes. I'm sorry. I'm here because we had an opening in the schedule and wanted to offer it to you first."

"The wedding has been called off," Margaret said, then picked her book back up, dismissing me.

"As in forever, or just until Claudine gets out of the hospital?"

She set the book back on the table and glanced at me again, obviously irritated. "*If* she gets out of the hospital. The prognosis isn't grand. What date opened up, if you don't mind me asking?"

"Oh yes," I said. "July—July Fifth."

"Is that so?" She narrowed her eyes.

"That's what Patricia told me when she asked me to rush over here."

"And that's the only date that's opened up this summer?"

"Oh yes," I said. "We're booked solid through August."

Margaret stared at me for a moment, then started laughing.

"So—um—did you want me to pencil you in?"

"You can drop the act, Shayla Murphy. I already know who you are."

13

My heart felt like it might beat out of my chest. Margaret Carragher knew I'd been lying straight to her face. I'd been made, and I hadn't even realized it.

"Oh, don't look so down," Margaret said. "Your act was good, but your face is everywhere. Just look at the women over there. They seem to be obsessed with you."

I glanced over to find the women at the other table glaring at me. All of them wore Anti-Shayla pins.

I tried to steady my breath.

"I suppose I owe you a hefty bit of gratitude." She pulled a chair out for me to sit beside her.

"Why is that?" I sat.

"You got rid of my problem."

"If you're talking about Claudine, I did no such thing."

"You don't have to keep up the façade with me. I know how horrible she was. If I had been in the country, I would have pushed her myself."

"You were out of the country?" I could feel my chest deflate.

"You didn't come here to see if I'd done it, did you?" She laughed as she realized that was precisely why I'd come. "That's a good one. I'd never murder someone with my own hands."

That didn't make me any less suspicious.

"Or hire anyone." Margaret waved a hand in the air. "Come on, don't be such a square. I'm not a murderer. I take care of problems the old-fashioned way."

"What's the old-fashioned way?"

"Digging up their dirt. Their secrets. Their past. Everyone has a past. Everyone has something they don't want their significant other to know." She took a sip of her water and sat back in her chair. "It was only a matter of time before I presented enough evidence to my son for him to dump his stripper girlfriend."

"I think he truly loves her," I said.

"If he did, would he spend every night at that ridiculous club where they met?" She shook her head. "Not a chance."

"If neither of us pushed her over that railing, who do you think did?" I asked. "Do you think Roland could—"

"Roland is as soft as his father," she interrupted. "In our family, the women do the dirty work."

"Is digging up dirt the only way you do the dirty work?"

"Dear girl, if I went around telling my secrets, they wouldn't be secret anymore, would they?" She reached for her book. "Now, if you'd kindly let me get back to my book? I was right in the middle of a spicy part."

I stood and turned.

"And next time you try to pretend you're someone else, make sure you have all the information correct."

I spun back around. "What did I have incorrect?"

"July Fifth is not the only available date before August at the Ballywick Castle," she said. "If you really worked for Patricia, you would have known that."

I avoided eye contact with the Anti-Shayla women and marched out of the dining room back to the lobby, where Seamus seemed to be finishing some business with the front desk attendant.

"Are you ready?" I asked as nicely as possible.

"Just as soon as yeh take a picture for yer membership," Seamus said.

My irritation with Patricia's lies about not having a date available before August dissipated a bit. "My membership?"

"I thought yeh might enjoy a visit now and then. Or daily. Whatever suits yer preference. It's all-inclusive."

I could only imagine how expensive an all-inclusive day spa membership was, but I didn't ask. "Thank you. That means a lot to me."

Seamus kissed me on the cheek, and the woman behind the desk smiled.

Once she'd taken my photo and given me my membership card, Seamus and I headed out of the lobby.

"What happened in there?" Seamus asked when we were free of eavesdroppers.

"She made me," I said. "She knew I was lying from the get-go."

"Ah, I'm sorry, love."

"I do know two things—one, she was out of the country when Claudine was murdered." I left out the part about her possibly hiring someone. If she'd hired someone, she likely wouldn't have just thrown it out there so willy-nilly. Or would she? "Two—Patricia lied to us about not having any additional dates before August. I think we should head over there and confront her about it."

Seamus checked his watch. "I must head back to Dublin to get Killian settled in his flat. Maybe we could go this evening?"

Patricia probably wouldn't be there after hours on a Thursday. "I can go talk to her myself. It'll be fine."

"Are yeh sure?" Hesitation edged Seamus' voice.

"I'll be on my best behavior."

"It's not you I'm worried about," Seamus said. "It's still possible whoever tried to kill Claudine was trying to kill you."

He had a point. "I'll be careful. I know how to handle myself." If there was one thing I had been good at in police academy, it was self-defense. My mother had drilled that into my brain my entire life.

"I know yeh do," Seamus said. "I'll call myself a separate car to take me to Dublin. You go in this one."

"Thank you," I said. "And thank you again for the membership here. I'm excited to use it."

"Make sure yeh do," Seamus said with a wink.

Ballywick Castle took my breath away every time I drove up the long shrub-lined driveway. Even though Roland had given us our June date, I still needed to figure out why Patricia had lied to me.

Maybe she was part of the Anti-Shayla Brigade. I had seen no sign of that in her office, but it would make sense by how she treated me.

Patricia sat at her desk, going through what looked like one of the bridal binders she put together for every client. "Shayla, I didn't expect to see you here today."

I told myself on the car ride I would be stern and not a pushover when I saw her, but I couldn't help the polite smile that betrayed my resolve. I quickly changed it back into a neutral face. "I have something I need to speak with you about."

"Please come in and have a seat. I'm always available to speak to my brides."

It would have been easier to be firm while standing, but I didn't want to appear confrontational. I still had to work with this woman until after the wedding.

Patricia pushed a button on the phone in front of her. "Could you please come in here?"

A different assistant than the one from the other day walked into her office and simply stood next to Patricia's desk like a guard dog.

Patricia interlaced her fingers in front of her. "What is it you needed to speak with me about?"

I steadied my breath and tried to speak slowly and clearly. "I know you were lying about having dates available before August."

14

Patricia considered me for a moment before she replied, "I don't know where you heard that, but I most definitely didn't lie to you."

"I spoke with Roland's mother today. She informed me you gave her several other options for the wedding date if Claudine wakes up."

"*When* Claudine wakes up," Patricia said. "We must think positively."

She wasn't answering my question. I sat in silence, allowing the awkwardness to do its job.

Patricia finally sat back in her chair and said, "I don't know what Roland's mother said, but there simply aren't any additional dates until later this year. She may have been goading you. She seems the type to do that. But may I offer my congratulations on getting the wedding date of your choice, even if it did come at the expense of another?"

Knife twisted. Ouch.

"I didn't hurt Claudine to get her wedding date," I said. "I wouldn't do that."

"You were pretty angry when you walked out of here that day."

"I was flustered. Not angry."

"Did you know Claudine is my boyfriend's sister?" Patricia frowned at me.

"I did not know that."

"She's also a very good friend of mine."

"So maybe the dates you provided were because of the friends and family bonus?"

Patricia slammed her hands on her desk and stood. Her guard assistant startled at her side.

"I didn't provide her with other dates," Patricia yelled. "There are no other dates. I don't know why Margaret lied to you, but she's horrible. She practically tortured Claudine. But Claudine is so stupidly in love with that man, she put up with it."

"What do you mean she tortured Claudine?" I practically whispered. I kept my butt in my seat to diffuse the tension in the room. If I stood and started shouting back, it would quickly lead to a much larger confrontation.

"Don't sit there and act like you think Margaret pushed her. She was out of the country. I'm sure she told you that when you talked to her this morning at the club." Patricia ran her hands down the front of her pink and white polka-dotted suit jacket, then sat back down. "Plus, we are all aware of who actually pushed Claudine."

I wouldn't defend myself to her any longer. "You can think what you want. But please tell me what you know about Margaret and Claudine's relationship."

"That garda told you to stay out of this. Maybe you should do as she says."

I groaned in frustration. "Please?"

"I have a meeting coming up. Call and schedule an appointment if you'd like to discuss the arrangements for your new date." She returned to reading the bridal book in front of her while her guard glared at me.

I took the hint and walked out of her office with less information than I thought I'd had when I walked in.

I took the long way back to the car—through the rear exit into the garden. Even though the flowers weren't in bloom yet, it was still beautiful with the lush green grass, ponds, and stone walls to keep guests from falling to their deaths over the cliffs.

I pulled my phone out of my purse to take a photo of the ocean view, the flowers, and the castle. I probably had a hundred pictures of the castle and its grounds, but it was so beautiful that I had a hard time not taking photos.

But even the surrounding beauty wasn't enough to get my mind off the case.

Who could it have been if neither Roland nor his mother had pushed Claudine? Maybe Roland had been cheating, and the other woman pushed her. Or Margaret hired someone to do the job.

I shook my head and sat on the rock wall. The ocean crashed below onto the massive rocks that looked like mere pebbles from this height. Roland seemed only to have eyes for Claudine. He hadn't wanted to be at the club at all. Was it possible she just slipped and fell over the edge?

Maybe when she said *ouch*, it was because she'd

twisted her ankle or something. But then what about the rest of it? The *what are you talking about* part? That wasn't something you just said to yourself.

But then who?

Or had someone really been gunning for me?

I glanced around to make sure no one had followed me. It would be relatively easy to push me over the cliff.

If someone had been trying to kill me, who could it have been? A member of the Anti-Shayla Brigade? Since I'd heard about it, I'd seen buttons everywhere. There had even been a couple of signs on people's properties on the way to the castle today.

Before I could consider it anymore, my phone rang in my hand—my mother's face on the screen. "Hello?"

"Shayla? Are you there?"

"I'm here," I said with the phone up to my ear. "What's up, mom?"

"I heard someone was killed at the castle where you're getting married."

This made me sit up straighter. "You were listening when I told you about the castle?" She hardly ever took in the details of my life, even though I felt compelled to tell her about them.

"You always make me out to be some kind of horrible mother," she said. "Of course, I remember where you're getting married."

"I don't think you're a horrible mother," I said. "You're just busy with your own wedding and those details."

"Speaking of the details, I've sent you my itinerary for the next year and a half."

"Your itinerary?" I almost laughed but knew it wouldn't go well if I did. "What do you mean?"

"Come on, don't you have an itinerary? You have so many fancy planners over there. I figured at least one of them would have created an itinerary."

"It's not like I'm going on a worldwide trip after my wedding. I don't really need an itinerary."

Mom huffed. "Do you want me to send it to you or not?"

"Yes, please send it," I said. "Is it set in stone, or is it fluid?"

"Stone," she said. "Nothing's changing. It's perfect the way it is."

"Good to know," I said. "Thanks for sending it."

"Now, about that woman who was murdered."

"She didn't die," I said. "She fell from a second-story balcony to the stone floor, but she's still alive."

"Or was pushed."

"That is possible."

"Are you worried about your safety?"

"No," I said, glancing over the cliffs. "I was here when it happened. I almost went to jail because they thought I did it."

Mom gasped, then whispered, "Did you?"

"Mother," I said in horror. "Of course, I didn't push someone over a balcony."

"Are the police investigating?"

"The Gardaí are looking into it."

"And what are you doing about it?"

"I'm looking into it as well."

"Good girl," Mom said.

A smile broached my face. I rarely received compliments from her about anything, let alone anything to do with police work.

"Make sure you look into the groom."

"I have."

"And the mother-in-law."

"She was out of the country."

"And what about an ex-boyfriend?"

"Good idea." I did a mental head slap. "That'll be my next stop. Thanks."

"If you need anything else, call me. I'd happily work through the investigation with you."

"Really?" I asked.

"Sure thing," Mom said. "I gotta go, kid. Take care."

She hung up, leaving me with a cautious sense of optimism.

The smile on my face didn't last long. As I watched the waves, something appeared on the rocks. Something that was not supposed to be there.

A body.

15

I started to call Molly but hesitated. What if she thought I was the one who'd pushed someone else over the cliff? I was the one standing right here.

But I couldn't just *not* report a body. It was unethical. Even if I ended up in handcuffs again.

"Molly," she said after one ring.

"It's Shayla," I said. "I think I found a body on the rocks below the cliff at Ballywick Castle."

At first, I thought I'd lost service because the other side of the line sounded like it had gone dead. But as I was pulling it away from my ear to check, she said, "You must be joking."

"I have fairly good vision," I said. "And from my view, it looks like a body."

She let out a loud sigh. "I'll be there as soon as I can." She disconnected the call without so much as a goodbye.

A voice startled me from behind as I slipped it back into my purse. "Miss Murphy?"

"You know, you shouldn't sneak up on people sitting on

the edge of a cliff." I turned to see a woman I recognized as the assistant who had been guarding Patricia in her office.

"I didn't mean to startle you," she said. "I need you to sign an updated contract now that you've changed your date."

"We didn't change our date. We just got our original date back," I said. "I would assume our contract would still be accurate."

She shrugged and handed me the paperwork. "Patricia said she needs a new one."

I quickly glanced through the paperwork but didn't recognize any differences. "Can I take this with me to have Seamus sign it too?"

"Sure," she said. "Just get it back ASAP."

"Is there any way I could get the original contract as well? I'd like to compare them to see what changes have been made."

"Patricia should have sent you a copy via email."

I opened my phone and searched for any emails from Patricia. I only had one with the original wedding planning questionnaire. "It looks like I didn't get it." I did a little pout. "Would it be too much trouble to get you to make me a copy or even send it again?"

She glanced over her shoulder at the castle entrance.

"You know what? Don't worry about it. I'll ask Patricia myself." I marched toward the door.

She hurried after me. "No. Stay away from her. I can do it."

I was almost at Patricia's office when the assistant put herself in front of me and held out both hands. "If you go in there," she whisper-yelled at me, "I'll have to resort to physical violence."

This took me aback. Was she physically threatening me now?

"Did you get the gold digger to sign the new contract, Anna?" Patricia called out from her office.

I tilted my head and raised my eyebrows at Anna. She seemed torn about what to do at this moment.

I peeked around the assistant and into Patricia's office. "You mean this gold digger?"

Patricia gaped at me from her desk. "You—I—but—"

"Yeah, I'm guessing I wasn't supposed to hear that, right?"

She didn't respond.

"Don't deny it," I said. "I'd guess there aren't many gold diggers you need to get to sign a new contract out here on a Thursday."

"I'm so sorry," Anna said, though I didn't know which one of us she was apologizing to.

"Come here," Patricia said.

Anna hurried to her side.

Patricia grabbed Anna's hand. For a second, I thought she was going to smack her or something. Instead, she simply opened Anna's palm and scribbled something on her hand. "Now, please give us a minute. And close the door."

Anna's eyes widened at Patricia's request. It was probably unusual that Patricia would be alone with a client in her office. But she did as was asked.

"You caught me," Patricia said. "I don't like you. But

whether I like you or not has nothing to do with my professionalism regarding your wedding."

"Professionalism, as in yelling out that one of your brides is a gold digger, so it echoes through the castle? That doesn't sound very professional to me."

"Come off it. What is it you want?"

This was my chance to ask about Claudine and whether she had any jilted exes. But first, I had to ask, "Why don't you like me?"

Patricia narrowed her eyes at me. "You tried to kill my friend."

"You didn't like me before Claudine went over that balcony."

"You've no proof of such a thing."

I sighed and went in another direction. "I want to know how Margaret was torturing Claudine and whether Claudine had any jilted exes."

"No way," Patricia said. "You're just trying to clear your name, even though it's obvious you're the one who did it."

"I can always have Gráinne O'Malley tell your boss what has transpired today." I kept my tone sugary sweet.

Patricia slumped in defeat. Now, she had to tell me. Though she likely wouldn't tell me everything, just enough to keep me from ratting her out.

"Margaret is mean and nasty and did everything she could to keep them apart."

"Specifics please?"

"When she found out Roland was going to ask Claudine to marry him, she showed up at the engagement and took back the ring handed down from his grandmother. She told Claudine she wasn't good enough to wear it."

Margaret seemed cold enough to do precisely that.

"Then she's had someone following them around to dig up dirt and report back to her so she can tell each of them what the other was doing. It's started quite a lot of arguments between them."

"Do you think Roland could have pushed Claudine over the balcony?"

She turned and looked out the window. "It's entirely possible."

"Why? What could Claudine have done to make him mad enough to push her over the balcony?"

Patricia turned back to me. "I'm not telling you the deepest, darkest secrets of one of my friends. Go ahead and get me fired. That's crossing a line."

"Then what about the exes? Did she have any exes who might have wanted her dead?"

"The only ex who might have wanted her dead was from years ago. He was abusive, and she got him sent to prison. It was a big deal around here. But he's probably still in prison. And he didn't have any money, so it's not like he could have hired someone to push Claudine." Her eyes widened. "Maybe Margaret hired someone to kill her."

I didn't point out the fact that she'd been convinced I had been the one who pushed Claudine only minutes before.

"What was his name?" I asked. "Just in case."

"Ivo Doyle."

"And what about Roland? Were there any exes that might have done this to get him back?"

She would have spit it all over her desk if she had been taking a drink. "Pssh, no way. Claudine's the first woman ever actually to enjoy his presence. They're both into the same niche movies and books. They truly are a good match, even if Margaret doesn't think so."

"That's all I have right now."

Patricia unclenched her jaw and relaxed slightly.

As I stood, I remembered the documents in my lap. "One more thing."

Patricia leaned forward. "What?"

"Can I please have a copy of our original contract so I can compare this one with that one? Or maybe you can explain to me how they differ?"

She reached across and yanked the paperwork out of my hand before I could stop her.

"Hey!" I said, but she was already ripping it to shreds. "That makes you look really suspicious, you know?"

"Suspicious of what?"

"Trying to trick me into signing something that's not above board."

"Prove it." She shoved the pieces into a shredder. "Now, you can see yourself out if you're finished."

"I forgot to mention," I said. "The gardaí are on their way. It seems there's a body at the bottom of the cliff just past the garden."

Patricia's eyes widened.

"Which means I'll probably be here just a bit longer."

When I walked out of Patricia's office, the guard assistant was talking to Molly.

"There you are," Molly said. "I haven't got all day. Show me what you saw."

It was apparent Molly hadn't told Patricia's assistant what business she had at the castle.

I motioned for her to follow me. As we were walking outside, I almost ran directly into a couple coming in with another white-uniformed assistant—one I'd never seen before.

"I'm sorry," I said, but they paid me no attention.

"I couldn't believe he asked me, and the first thing I wanted to do was book this castle," the bride said. "Did you know all the O'Malleys get married here?"

The assistant shrugged and smiled as if I wasn't standing right there. Though she probably didn't know who I was.

"We want the soonest date possible," the groom said. "I can't wait to be married to this amazing woman."

I laughed to myself. They'd be super disappointed when they found out the earliest possible opening was in November.

"It's just over the wall," I said to Molly, pointing to where I'd been sitting when I saw the body.

She pulled out a pair of binoculars and walked to the edge. Within seconds Molly said, "It's a body. Looks like it's been down there a while. The saltwater affects that sort of thing." She shook her head. "How do you manage to come across all these things?"

I shrugged. "Maybe I'm more observant than most?"

She muttered a response that I couldn't hear. "You can go home. I'll take it from here."

I texted Seamus the minute I got in the car. Normally, I would have called him, but I knew he was in meetings, so I wrote him the longest text message known to man and pressed send.

The first thing I needed to do was find out if Ivo Doyle was still in prison. Then I needed to devise a plan to determine if Margaret had hired someone to kill Claudine. My guess: that was way above my abilities and resources, but sometimes there were workarounds.

"Can you please take me to the pub in Ballywick?" I asked the driver as we pulled out of the parking lot.

It was then that I noticed the beat-up junker following closely behind us. A man sat in the driver's seat wearing a hat and sunglasses.

I kept a close eye on him as we made our way to town,

but when we turned toward the pub, I said to the driver, "I think we're being followed."

He nodded. "I noticed that too. I'll make a few turns to make sure."

The junker followed us through three of the four turns, heading in a different direction on the last one. Either he had been simply going into town the same way we were, or he realized we saw him following.

"Do you want me to come into the pub just in case he shows up?" the driver asked when he pulled up in front of Harry's—the hub of the town.

"I'll be okay," I said. "But thanks."

Harry greeted me when I walked in. "Shayla, what's the craic?"

"Nothing good, Harry, nothing good." I shook my head and sat at the bar. "Can I get a Guinness, please?"

"Is this about that nonsense going around that you pushed that lady out of a car?"

"First a roof, now a car." I couldn't stop myself from laughing.

"You pushed someone off a roof, too?" Harry looked at me, stunned.

"I didn't push anyone off anything," I said. "Technically, Claudine fell from a second-story balcony."

"Makes more sense why she would have pulled through." Harry smiled. "And don't yeh be worryin'. I'd never think yeh capable of hurtin' someone. Yer too sweet." He put the Guinness in front of me.

"Who's been talking about me?" I asked before taking a sip of the beer.

"No one in particular," Harry said. "Just the gossip roaming around. Can yeh tell me what really happened?"

I shook my head. "I don't know. Someone pushed her. I'm almost certain. But I don't know who. Did you know Claudine?"

He shrugged and began wiping down the bar. "She came in once or twice."

The tone of his voice and his inability to look me in the eye gave him away. "Is that the only place you saw her?"

His face flushed. "I'm a man, yeh know. Maybe I saw her a time or two at the club. Means nothing."

"Did you know her ex?" I asked. "The one who went to prison?"

"Ivo? I think he recently got out."

"How recently?" I asked, my heart rate increasing.

"Last week or so." Harry's eyes lit up as if a switch had turned on a lightbulb in his head. "Yeh think he had something to do with it?"

"He was in prison for domestic violence, wasn't he?"
Harry nodded.

"Do you know where he lives?" I pulled out my phone to wait for an address.

"Yeh won't be needing your phone," Harry said. "His mam lives in the apartment above the pizzeria. I'd bet me left arm he's staying with her."

I chugged the rest of the Guinness and set the empty glass on the bar. "Thanks for the chat." I slid him a ten-euro note. "Keep the change."

"Don't tell him I told yeh were to find him," Harry said. "Gotta keep me anonymity."

I gave him a thumbs up before walking out into the fading sunlight. I told my driver where I was headed and started walking.

I'd never eaten at the pizzeria before, but the smell wafting from the tiny shop was delightful. Their signs boasted of their thick crust and quick delivery times.

To the right of the pizzeria door was a smaller glass door with a set of stairs to the upstairs apartment. I rang the doorbell, and a buzzer sounded.

"Does that mean I can come upstairs?" I asked into the tiny speaker box.

"What else would it mean?" a woman asked, her voice low and crackly.

I turned the knob and pushed the door open before walking up the steep staircase.

The single door to the apartment was open when I got to the top.

"Put the pizza on the counter. The money's all there," the woman said.

Sure enough, there were several notes on the counter amongst what looked like a month's worth of mail and takeout menus.

"I'm not a pizza delivery person," I said. "I'm here to speak with Ivo."

"What would yeh be needing with my son?" A large woman in a dressing gown hobbled out of another room, kicking stray boxes and pieces of trash out of her path.

"I'd like to ask him some questions," I said. "About Claudine."

She narrowed her eyes. "I already know what yer thinking, but he had nothing to do with her fall. He was already wrongly accused once. I won't let my baby go back to prison again."

"I'm not accusing him of anything," I said. "I just want to know more about Claudine. To see if he might know who could have wanted her dead."

She let out a ragged laugh. "Just about anyone who knew Claudine would want that girl dead."

"Why do you say that?"

"She's a manipulative, gold-digging stripper," Ivo's mother said. "She and Ivo were together for years—engaged even—until she made up some horrible story about him to get Roland's sympathy. And Roland was just stupid enough to think a woman like that would have any interest in such a rat like him. He helped put Ivo in prison. I can't help but think he's not too happy they cleared Ivo of all charges."

I felt my jaw drop. "How was he cleared of the charges?"

"I hired someone to do some digging," she said. "Brilliant girl and cheap, too. She found records of Claudine's actual location the nights she claimed Ivo attacked her."

"I'm guessing she wasn't with Ivo?"

She smiled a gummy smile. "Nope. She was working at that other club. The one Roland didn't know about."

Another club? Now we were getting somewhere. "And when did all of this become public?"

"Last week. Which I'm guessing is why Roland pushed her over that balcony."

I needed to speak to Roland again. He'd have no choice but to talk to me when I brought this information to his attention.

"Can you tell me where Ivo is so I can talk to him about this? I think he may have more information."

She shook her head. "Yer not getting close to my son. The minute he got out of prison, he went to America. Hasn't been back since. And if yeh don't believe me, I can show yeh the tracking record I have on his phone."

I bowed out as gracefully as possible, almost running into the pizza delivery guy as I made my way down the stairs.

17

The cottage was warm and welcoming when I hurried through the doors. "Seamus? Are you home?"

No response.

It wasn't terribly strange living with Seamus since we'd practically been living together since we started dating, but what caught me off guard nearly every time I walked through the cottage was the reminder that it was ours. Our home. My home. This gorgeous home on a gorgeous property with gorgeous furnishings was mine.

Like many little girls, I had always dreamt of being a princess. That my father was a king in some far-off country who would show up on my sixteen birthday and whisk me off into my royal duties.

But sixteen passed. Then eighteen and twenty. When my twenty-first birthday came and went, my hopes of being a princess had evaporated.

Now gratitude overwhelmed me, stealing my breath away every time I walked through the door. I may not have a tiara or a kingdom to rule, but my fantasy of becoming a princess had practically come true.

A snorting sound came from the back door, drawing a smile to my lips. I hurried to the kitchen to grab an apple and then rushed outside to greet Cupid. "Hello, Darling." I handed him the apple, and he happily nibbled on it while it rested in my palm. "Have you been a good boy today?"

He finished the apple and neighed loudly.

"Are you certain?"

He neighed again and wiggled his lips open to show me his teeth. I didn't know horses very well yet, but I took this as a smile.

"I'm glad," I said. "I had a challenging day—lots of dead ends and unanswered questions. Everyone in town thinks I tried to kill a woman because she took my wedding date. I didn't, though. I'd have never pushed someone over a balcony. You know that, don't you?"

Cupid nuzzled his adorable face into my chest as I sucked in a deep breath and closed my eyes.

We stayed in that position for a few minutes before I heard the back door to the cottage open and footsteps approaching.

"There you are," Seamus said.

I turned and kissed him. "How was work?"

He beamed. "It was grand. I don't know why I was so keen to leave the family business behind. I love it."

"That's fantastic," I said. "I'm so happy you're happy."

"I only just got yer message on the way here. I can't believe Patricia would be so horrible to yeh. I'll have me mother—"

"Not yet," I said. "Right now, she's on my side. She knows I have the upper hand."

"Have yeh heard anything about the body?"

I shook my head. "I don't expect I will. It's not like Molly is keen to have me on her investigations."

"Speaking of, any news on the case?" Seamus and I sat on a couple of wicker chairs with fluffy, water-resistant cushions.

"I know Roland acted like he had nothing to do with it, but I'm starting to wonder if he did," I said. "Either that or his mother hired someone."

Seamus nodded, listening.

"One of Claudine's exes was in prison for domestic violence and just got out a week or so ago."

Seamus' eyebrows lifted.

"But according to his mother, he went straight to America and hasn't returned since."

"Grand," Seamus said. "I know how much yeh love dead ends."

"It boils down to Roland and his mom as suspects. We know for certain Roland was there when it happened. I'm pretty confident he and Claudine were fighting about either him still going to the strip clubs or her still working at them."

"Wait, she's still working at strip clubs?"

"That's what Patricia told me."

"Have yeh completely ruled out the possibility that someone thought Claudine was you?"

I considered it. "Not completely. But there are either too many or too few people who want me dead. I don't have any outright enemies and there seem to be quite a lot of Anti-Shayla Brigade members. Have you gotten any more threatening letters?"

"Not that I'm aware of." He reached over and grabbed my hand in his. "What's your next step?"

"I need to talk to Roland, even if he doesn't want to talk to me," I said. "I just have to find him."

"Since they tossed him out of the club the other night, he's been at the hospital with Claudine."

"Do you want to go with me?" I asked, standing.

Cupid neighed loudly.

I turned and laughed. "You can't go, Silly."

He pawed at the ground.

Seamus put an arm around my shoulders. "Let's go catch some bad guys."

Claudine's room was on the third floor and, sure enough, Roland was asleep in one of the uncomfortable-looking chairs next to Claudine's bed. The sound of an audiobook playing in the room was barely audible over the sound of the ventilator and beeping machines that reminded everyone Claudine was still alive, even if she wasn't conscious.

As we tiptoed into the room, another person came into view—Patricia. And the source of the audiobook. Except it wasn't a recording, it was Patricia reading softly to Claudine.

When Patricia caught a glimpse of us out of the corner of her eye, she dropped the book on the floor and waved her arms in the air as if she might try to ninja chop one of us. As she realized who we were, she dropped her hands to her sides, but the look on her face was more vicious than her flailing had been.

I reached down and picked up the book—the same one Margaret had been reading with the naked man chest—before handing it to Patricia.

She snatched it from my hands and hissed, "Don't judge. It's for book club. What are you doing here?"

"We wanted to talk to Roland," Seamus said.

"Let the poor man have some peace," she said. "The gardaí have been questioning him all day."

If only I could have called Molly and asked her what she'd found out, this process might go more smoothly. Maybe I'd try tomorrow, especially if I discovered some information I could use to help her.

"Have they questioned you yet?" Patricia asked, narrowing her eyes at me.

I shook my head.

"Must be nice to be rich," she muttered.

"Roland's family is rich too," Seamus said. "Didn't get him off the hook, did it?"

"He's the partner," Patricia whisper yelled. "The partner always gets questioned. Even if they had nothing to do with it."

"Earlier today, you practically said he was the killer," I said.

"I appreciate the vote of confidence," Roland said from his chair.

"I was just trying to get her out of my office," Patricia said pleadingly. "I was saying anything I could to—"

"Whatever," Roland said, holding up a hand to shush

her. "Shayla heard us arguing. At least that gives her probable cause to suspect me."

Patricia looked somewhere between angry and worried.

Roland stood. "Stay with Claudine. I need to have a chat with Seamus and Shayla."

18

Seamus and I shared a glance and shrugged before following Roland out the door.

"Look, I'm going to say this once more so everyone will get off my back," Roland said as we walked down the hall toward the elevator. "I already told the gardaí. Now I'm telling you."

I wanted to shout—*get on with it already. Enough with the theatrics.* But I held my tongue.

"Claudine and I were arguing about our time in the club. She was still stripping, and I was still attending. Not her club because I didn't know where she was working but at the one in Dublin from the other night."

We walked into the elevator, and he pushed the ground floor button.

Was he using a story to walk us out of the building?

"My mother had someone digging around in our business and told each of us what the other was doing. She wanted us to split, but nothing could have split us up.

Even with all our indiscretions, we still loved each other. We would have worked it out."

Seamus and I stood in silence, waiting for Roland to continue his story.

"The rest, I've already told yeh," he said.

When he led us out of the elevator, I expected him to walk us to the door, but instead, he went in the opposite direction.

We hesitated, and he stopped. "I'd like to get some coffee from the cafeteria while we speak if that's okay?"

Seamus looked at me before nodding. We followed him in silence to the cafeteria, where we all ordered lattes and sat in a couple of armchairs near the large windows overlooking the parking lot.

"Did you see anyone else go upstairs? Either before or after you and Claudine fought?" I asked.

Roland looked down at his coffee. "No."

"The only way we can help find who did this is by knowing the whole truth." I was gentle with my words, trying to coax him into honesty.

At first, it seemed he wouldn't say anything else, but then he looked up. "The PI was there. The one my mother keeps on the payroll."

"Did yeh see him go upstairs?" Seamus asked.

"No, but he's sneaky. And he does whatever my mother tells him to do."

I tilted my head a bit. "Anything?"

He nodded. "Anything."

This was not the first time he'd alluded to his mother hiring someone to hurt Claudine.

"Of course, I don't want to think that about me own

mam," he said. "But when the facts are staring me right in the eyes, it's hard to turn me head."

"I assumed you'd think I did it," I said. "That's what the gardaí thought—think."

"I know yeh didn't push her," Roland said. "I saw yeh on the third floor before I went to the jacks. There's no way you could have gotten down to the second floor by the time I heard her scream."

I sat forward. "Did you tell this to the gardaí?"

"Sure did," he said with a half-smile. "It's probably why you're not locked up right now."

I could feel Seamus' gaze, but I didn't glance at him. He and I both knew why I hadn't been arrested, but maybe Roland's interview had kept me out of jail.

Roland pulled his vibrating phone from his pocket and rolled his eyes at whoever was calling. "Yes?" As he listened, his face changed from frustration to worry. "Grand. We'll be right there."

He stood, then looked back at Seamus and me, still sitting at the table.

"Me mam's upstairs, causing a ruckus with Patricia. We need to hurry."

Seamus and I ran to keep up.

The shouts were clear the moment the elevator doors opened.

A nurse stood just outside Claudine's doorway with a petrified look on her face.

"Call security," Roland said to her before pushing past and into the room. "What are the two of yeh doin'? Yer makin' a holy show of yerselves!"

On either side of Claudine's bed were Margaret and

Patricia, screaming over a woman who may or may not hear them.

"I told you already, you're not welcome here," Patricia shouted. "Get out!"

"This is none of your business. She was to be my future daughter-in-law."

"She was to be my future sister-in-law."

"Funny, I haven't seen her brother here to sit by her bed. Only you."

"He's been busy." Patricia's eyes flashed to me, then narrowed. "What are you doing here? I thought you were leaving."

I stepped into the room. "I was just talking to Roland about what happened that day."

"Like you don't know," Patricia said.

"She didn't do it," Roland said. "I already told yeh that."

"How much did she pay you to say that?"

Roland looked at her as if what she'd said was a joke. "I don't believe I need the money."

Patricia—realizing her mistake—waved a hand in the air. "Then maybe she did something else to get you to lie to the gardaí."

"Don't even," I said. "I did nothing of the sort, nor would I. I'm innocent, and I'm going to prove who did it."

"Don't look at me," Margaret said. "I was out of the country, remember?"

I wasn't about to show her my cards yet. I needed to find and talk to the PI she had working for her first. "Maybe so, maybe not. I'm sure the gardaí are looking carefully into your travel."

Margaret straightened herself and tucked a piece of stray hair behind her ear before throwing her purse over her shoulder and making her way toward the door.

Roland stepped to the side to let her by, but just as Margaret passed Patricia, Patricia dove at her.

Margaret seemed ready for the attack as they pulled each other's hair, kicked at each other with their stiletto heels, and ended up toppling over onto Claudine.

"Stop!" Seamus, Roland, and I all shouted at once.

The contents of Margaret's purse went flying everywhere.

We hurried to pull the two women off Claudine. She was helpless in her bed, just trying to survive. She didn't need people rolling around on top of her.

Once we got them off Claudine, Roland pulled his mother away by her waist, and I held onto Patricia.

"Let go of me," Margaret growled. "She attacked me. I'm calling the Gardaí."

"Go for it. It was worth it." Patricia steadied herself with a malicious grin on her face.

Margaret started cleaning up the things that had fallen on the floor.

Seamus, Roland, and I helped her pick up while Patricia glared at us. I kept an eye on her in case she went for round two.

Before returning to a stand, I handed Margaret a pair of driving gloves and a lipstick tube.

"What is this?" Roland held up a small wooden box. "You still have this in your purse?"

"Come off it. I haven't had a chance to go to the bank."

"It's been nearly three weeks," he said.

"Don't go getting any ideas," she said. "I told you once, and I'll tell you again—that woman will not be getting my family ring."

She ripped the box out of his hand and shoved it in her purse before storming out of the room.

Moments later, three nurses and two security guards rushed in and started speaking at once.

"Everyone out."

"Who turned off the machine?"

"How did this get pulled out?"

"The monitor alarms are silenced."

"Clear!"

Before I turned to leave, I saw them put the paddles on Claudine's chest and send electricity through her body to get her heart rhythm back to normal.

Her body jolted.

"Charge again! Clear!"

19

Roland paced the hallway as Patricia watched.

Back and forth, back and forth.

With every step he took, her eyes blinked.

The door to Claudine's room remained firmly closed, keeping us in the dark about what was happening.

I thought back to what the nurses had been yelling about the last few moments before we'd been escorted out of the room. The monitor volume had been silenced, something had been pulled out, and a machine had been turned off.

Could that have all happened while Patricia and Margaret had been fighting? Or had someone done that before we went into the room? If they'd silenced the monitor, we wouldn't have known that Claudine was in trouble, but the nurses would have.

"Did you leave Claudine's room while we were gone?" I whispered to Patricia.

She turned and glared at me.

"I'm just wondering if someone happened to sneak in

while you were gone and unplugged Claudine's machines or if that happened when you and Margaret were fighting."

"We couldn't have done that," Patricia hissed. "We only landed on her for a moment."

I shrugged. "You landed on her pretty hard, though."

"Only because Margaret pushed me."

"Did you leave the room at all?"

She huffed. "For a moment. I had to go to the loo."

"Was there anyone in the room when you got back?"

She turned to look down the hallway where Margaret stood talking on her cell phone. "Margaret was there. Maybe she did it."

It would only make sense that if she'd tried to kill Claudine once and had failed, she might have tried again.

A chill ran down my spine.

"Thanks," I said to Patricia.

She went back to watching Roland pace.

I squeezed Seamus' hand. "I'm going to talk to Margaret."

He nodded and turned to watch Roland pacing.

I inched my way down the hallway to speak to Margaret. When she saw me from the corner of her eye, she abruptly finished her phone call and returned her phone to her purse. "Can I help you?"

"Did you pull the plug on Claudine?" I asked.

She seemed taken aback by my question. "Pull the plug? As in literally?"

I stood in silence, studying her. If anything, she was likely a good liar when she needed to be.

"How do you believe I would have gotten away with that when Patricia never leaves the room?"

"Not even to go to the restroom?"

"The only times she leaves is when she has to work," Margaret said. "And then she's right back here."

"So you didn't go into an empty room with Claudine when you arrived?"

"I haven't been alone with Claudine since before her fall. And even then, I tried to avoid her at all costs."

One of them was lying, and I had a feeling it was the woman standing in front of me. Proving it would be the tricky part.

My mind returned to the gloves that had fallen from Margaret's purse. Could she have worn them to pull the plug so she wouldn't have left fingerprints?

I was about to ask when the doors to Claudine's room burst open.

"Is she okay?" Roland asked, rushing to the nurses.

"What happened? Will she survive?" Patricia asked.

The main nurse held up both of her hands to stop them. "She's stable again, but no one is allowed in that room right now."

"But—"

"No one," she repeated. "Not until each of you speaks with the gardaí."

"The gardaí?" Seamus asked. "Why do we need to speak with the gardaí?"

"Whatever happened in there was not by accident," the nurse said.

"And you think one of us had something to do with it?" Patricia asked, a look of irritation on her face.

"It would seem so," the nurse said. "But I'm not an investigator, just a lowly nurse who knows when patients have been tampered with."

"What do you mean, tampered with?" I asked.

"That's enough questions out of yeh lot," she said. "I have other patients to attend to. No one leaves until the gardaí arrive."

A guard stood in front of Claudine's door with his arms crossed over his chest.

"A nurse can't order me to stay here," Margaret said, swinging her purse onto her shoulder. "I'm leaving."

She marched down the hall to the elevators as we all watched.

Almost frantically, she pushed the down button, but when the doors opened, Molly led a group of gardaí officers out.

Whatever Molly said to Margaret had her changing directions and walking back toward us.

"This is absurd," Margaret said, the volume of her voice increasing. "I wouldn't be stupid enough to try to kill someone in a hospital with all the people around and the cameras and everything."

I looked up. There were cameras on the ceiling. Maybe they'd give away what happened.

When Molly's eyes landed on me, she sighed. "Why are you here?"

"I wanted to talk to Roland," I said.

She shook her head, obviously irritated with me. "I need to speak to each of you individually. Who would like to start?"

"I have places to be," Margaret said. "Start with me."

Molly nodded and took Margaret into a room labeled family lounge and securely closed the door.

I meandered over to the nurse station.

"Is there something you need?" the nurse who had told us not to leave asked.

"Do those cameras work?" I pointed to the cameras on the ceiling.

"Course they do," she said. "Why would we have them if they didn't work?"

"Are there cameras in the rooms?"

She shook her head. "Privacy and all."

"Couldn't the gardaí just access the cameras to see who was in the room when whatever was unplugged was unplugged?"

Her eyes darkened. "It was unplugged when all of you were in there. That's why we came rushing in."

My stomach felt like it flipped over. "It happened while we were in the room? How?"

"Why don't you tell me?"

"Could it have been an accident?" I asked. "There was a bit of a physical altercation. Could that have caused it?"

"It's possible, but not probable."

"Which side of the bed would you have had to be on to unplug whatever it was?"

"Could have been either side," she said. "The monitor alarms had to have been turned off on the far side, but the other things could have happened from either side."

That didn't help me at all.

"That's all I'm going to tell you," she said. "I have work to do."

"Thank you for the information."

I walked back down the hall where the guard stood watching Roland, Patricia, and Seamus as they waited outside the family lounge.

"What did the nurse say?" Roland asked.

I shook my head. "She wouldn't tell me anything." I wasn't about to tell them what I'd found out.

The family lounge door burst open, and Margaret marched out and down the hall without turning to look at us.

"Who's next?" Molly asked, rubbing the back of her neck.

20

Patricia and Roland went before Seamus and me. Patricia spent the most time talking to Molly and another garda. When Seamus was done, Molly had dark circles under her eyes.

"I'll wait for you in the car," Seamus said, giving me a quick kiss before I walked into the family lounge and sat on one of the worn couches.

"Can you start from the moment you arrived at the hospital?" Molly asked, not bothering with formalities.

"Do I need an attorney?" I asked.

"You're not under arrest," Molly said. "We just want to figure out what happened."

I told her everything I remembered in short order, then explained what the nurse had told me.

"I spoke with her on the way here," Molly said. "She told me the same thing. Do you have any clue of who might have done this?"

"If I had to guess," I said. "I'd put my money on Margaret. She hates the idea of Roland being with Claudine. I wouldn't put it past her to have hired someone to push Claudine from the balcony. Then, when Claudine didn't die, Margaret might have taken things into her own hands. Especially because if Claudine wakes up, she'll be able to identify who pushed her."

Molly sat forward in her chair. "Why would you think she'd be able to identify the person who pushed her?"

"Because she spoke to them, which means they likely said something to her first."

"She spoke to them?"

"Well, screamed at them," I said. "Whatever they said to her seemed to confuse her. I think she said something like *what are you talking about* as she fell."

Molly sat up straighter in her seat. "Why didn't you tell us this before?"

I scrunched up my face. "I thought I had."

"I would have remembered."

"Well, my guess is whoever tried to push—or hired someone to push—her is the same person who tried to kill her tonight. If tonight wasn't just an accident."

"From the fight?"

I nodded. "The nurse said it's not probable, but it was possible it could have happened accidentally."

Molly took down a couple of notes, then looked back at me. "Do you think it's possible Patricia or Roland had something to do with this?"

I considered this for a moment. "It doesn't seem like it. Patricia seems even more protective of Claudine than Roland. When we arrived, she was reading a book to Claudine. Apparently, she's been here every hour of the day when she's not working. If she was going to do something like this, why would she have waited until the room was full of people?"

"To take the spotlight off herself?"

"Possibly. But it just seems unlikely. They were really good friends since Claudine's brother is Patricia's boyfriend."

Molly furrowed her brow and flipped through her notes. She leaned over to her colleague, who shook his head almost imperceptibly.

"Where did you hear that Claudine's brother is Patricia's boyfriend?" Molly asked.

"Patricia told me. I highly doubt she would push one of her good friends and future sisters-in-law off a balcony. Which leaves us with either Margaret or Roland. And I don't think Roland did it."

She narrowed her eyes at me. "Are the two of you simply covering for one another?"

I sighed. "If that's what you think, then why am I even here answering your questions? Shouldn't I be in cuffs? Or shouldn't he?"

Molly's phone beeped from her pocket. She pulled it out, glanced at the screen, then returned it before saying, "That's all the questions we have for you."

She stood so abruptly her colleague startled.

"You may go," Molly said. "If you have any more information, please let us know."

Molly left the room and headed directly for the elevator.

I hurried after her and slipped into the elevator just before the doors closed. "Is everything okay? Why the rush?"

She didn't respond.

"Does it have something to do with the body at the bottom of the cliff?"

"They're still processing the scene," Molly said. "I haven't heard anything. Probably a jumper."

My stomach tightened. If her rush wasn't about the body, had there been another murder? But if that was the case, why had she left her colleague on the third floor without so much as an explanation?

When we reached the bottom floor, instead of heading toward the exit doors, she turned and practically ran toward the ER entrance.

I followed, my curiosity getting the better of me.

Molly stopped at the desk. "My daughter—they're bringing her in by ambulance."

The desk attendant pointed to the door, where two medics hurried in with what looked like a tiny person on a gurney.

"Sweetie, are you okay?" Molly asked, grabbing her daughter's hand.

I stayed back so as not to interrupt the moment. I was about to turn around when Molly shifted out of the way, and I got a full view of the little girl's face.

She was the spitting image of her parent, and that parent was not Molly.

My head spun as dizziness took over.

How was it even possible?

The math didn't work out in my head. Numbers bounced around like ping-pong balls.

Before I could work out the equation, darkness took over.

I must have only been out for a few seconds because when I regained consciousness, Molly was still standing where she'd been before, holding her daughter's hand.

Realization crossed Molly's face as she looked from me to her daughter and back again. She narrowed her eyes at me but didn't have time to say anything before the medics started off again, wheeling her daughter back behind two massive swinging doors.

A nurse I hadn't registered as being at my side squeezed my shoulder. "Are you okay? You hit your head pretty hard."

"I'm okay," I said, trying to sit up. When I did, it felt like all the blood rushed to my head, causing the pressure to intensify.

"Whoa, maybe you should get up slowly," she said. "Are you here with anyone?"

The thought of Seamus sitting in the car completely

clueless made me nauseous. Or maybe that was the concussion from smacking my head on the tile floor.

"My fiancé is in the car," I said. "In the parking lot—er—car park."

"What does his car look like?" She stood as if about to hurry out.

"Why don't I just call him?" I said, pulling out my phone.

"Good idea."

When Seamus answered, my throat went so dry that I could hardly make out any words. "I need you to come to the ER desk."

"Are yeh all right?" The car door slammed in the background.

"I fell and hit my head. I'm okay."

Within less than a minute, he was running toward me. I hung up the phone and covered my eyes with my arm. The light made my head pound even more.

"What happened to her?" Seamus asked the nurse.

"She seems to have fainted," the nurse answered. "Hit her head pretty badly on the floor. Probably has a concussion."

Exhaustion swept over me like a warm blanket.

"Shayla, you need to stay awake," Seamus' voice seemed far away.

I yawned. "I'm so sleepy."

"Do yeh think we need to have her admitted?" Seamus asked someone. I couldn't remember who.

"I think that'd be for the best," a woman said.

Someone shook my shoulders.

"Stay awake," Seamus said.

"I can't," I said. "I'm so tired."

When I woke again, Seamus sat sleeping in a chair similar to the one Patricia had been in next to Claudine's bed.

I glanced around. I was in a hospital bed just like Claudine's.

I tried to rewind what had happened. Seamus had come in, and I was tired. I'd fallen and hit my head. Molly was there. And—

I gasped, startling Seamus awake.

"What? What is it? Are yeh okay?"

Did he know? Had he been keeping it from me? Or had she been keeping it from him?

I had to tell him. "Seamus, before I fell—"

"Hey," Molly said, peeking into the room. "Can I talk to Shayla for a minute?"

Seamus glanced at me to see what I wanted.

"That's fine," I said.

He nodded and walked toward the door, whispering something to Molly before exiting.

Molly hesitantly sat in the chair Seamus had just vacated. "I'll explain everything, but yeh have to promise not to tell Seamus."

Part of me exhaled in relief that he didn't know, and the other part of me flared in his defense. "How could you keep it from him? He has a daughter."

"I didn't think he'd ever come back," she said. "I was going to tell him. I swear it."

"When?"

"When the time was right," she said, a vulnerability in her eyes I'd never seen before. "I don't know."

"You have to tell him."

"What if he tries to take her from me?"

My heart shattered for her. "He'd never do that."

"She's me whole world," Molly said. "I don't know what I'd do if—"

"He will not try to take your daughter away from you," I said. "But I'm sure he'd like to have a relationship with her. How old is she?"

"Six."

"That's six years he hasn't been part of," I said. "It's so unfair that you haven't told him."

"I thought I was doing what was best at the time," she said. "I thought I had a miscarriage, and then everything went arseways between Seamus and me. I came back and found out I was still with child. He'd made it very clear he didn't want to come back to Ireland, and there was no way I would go back to the states."

She'd made an impossible decision, even so, the wrong one. "Seamus is an amazing man. He will make an amazing father." I choked up on the last words. I'd only ever thought of him being an amazing father to *my* children—our children—and now I find out he has a child with someone else.

My head felt fuzzy again.

"Are yeh okay?" Molly asked.

"I'm fine," I said. "Is your daughter okay?"

"It was just a broken finger. She'll be just fine."

"What's her name?" I asked, trying to take deep breaths and not pass out again.

Molly hesitated.

"You don't have to tell me if you don't want to," I said.

Eventually, I'd know because there was no way I wasn't telling Seamus he had a daughter.

"Lila," she said. "Her name is Lila."

"Pretty name."

"Are yeh going to tell him?" Molly asked.

"I can't keep this from him," I said. "We tell each other everything."

She gave me a sideways glance.

"Maybe he kept some things from me initially, but that was just to protect himself." I held back from saying he was trying to protect himself from women like Molly, who only wanted him for his money.

Though, now, I was seeing her in a different light. If she'd only wanted him for his money, she easily could have gotten child support from him. And probably a lot of it.

"Just give me a little time to figure out how to break it to him," she said.

"How much time?"

"A month?"

"A week."

"Two weeks?"

"One," I said. "And sooner is preferable. If you don't tell him within a week, I will."

"One week," she said. "Consider it done."

How I'd manage to keep it from him for a week was beyond me.

"Also, I need to speak to yeh about the person yeh saw at the bottom of the cliffs." Molly shifted in the chair, pulling out her phone. "I just received some photos from the scene. It looks like the person who died worked at the castle."

She turned her phone screen to me, and the room spun.

The white uniform. The strong build. The snake tattoo.

"She was there the same day Claudine fell," I said.

"That's what I suspected." Molly swiped to show me another photo, this one a closeup of the woman's stained white pants.

"What am I looking at exactly?"

"Right there, on her pants, is what looks like a blood stain." Molly pointed at the stain.

"Are you certain it's not just mud?"

"It's being tested as we speak, but if it's Claudine's blood, we may have just found her killer."

22

"Are yeh certain yer okay?" Magella asked as she helped get me settled into bed after I'd arrived home the next day. Seamus had insisted the hospital keep me overnight for monitoring.

"I'm doing great," I said. "Thank you for your help."

She smiled and turned to Seamus. "Don't yeh be worrying. I'll take good care of her while yer away."

Seamus had several important meetings to attend. "Call me if the results come back on the stain on the pants, okay?"

"I will," I said.

"Take care of yerself today. Don't push it too hard. It looks like they caught the killer, so there's nothing for yeh to worry about." He leaned down and kissed me gently as if I might break at the slightest touch of his lips.

After he'd gone and Magella started tidying the rest of the cottage, I pulled out my cell phone and called Ivo Doyle's mom.

"Who is this?" she spat into the phone without so much as a hello.

"This is Shayla," I said. "We met the other day when I was asking about Claudine."

"I already told yeh, me boy's in America where no one can hurt him."

"Right," I said. "I'm actually calling about the woman you talked about who helped him get out of jail. I'd like to get her number from you, if possible."

She was only too happy to pass along the information.

"Thank you so much."

"Happy to help." She hung up without a goodbye.

I immediately called Telly.

"Telly," she said on the second ring. I noticed her distinct lack of an Irish accent. She was from the states—probably somewhere in the middle, like Iowa or Nebraska.

"Hi, Telly," I said. "My name is Shayla Murphy. Ivo Doyle's mother gave me your number and said you have a way with computers."

"What do you need me to hack?"

Straight to the point. I liked that. "A hospital's CCTV footage."

"Easy peasy," she said. "That'll be five hundred euros."

"Done," I said.

The phone sounded like it fell to the ground before she said, "Sorry about that. My hands are full, and I dropped the phone."

My guess was she hadn't expected me to go for the five hundred euros so readily.

"How quickly do you need the footage?"

"As quickly as you can get it." I gave her the details about which hospital and the date and time.

"I'll have it to you by the end of the day. Would you like me to deliver it in person or digitally?"

"In person would be great," I said. "Then I can pay you straight away."

I gave her the address to the cottage, and we disconnected the call.

Anxiety welled inside me. Keeping a secret from Seamus had been ridiculously difficult, even for the short time I'd had to keep it.

I pushed my way out of bed and went into the kitchen. Magella wasn't anywhere to be seen, which sent a bit of relief through me. I didn't need her telling me I couldn't be out of bed right now. What I needed was to busy my mind.

I needed to bake.

***

"Holy cakes," Seamus said when he walked in the door after several hours. "Is everything all right, love?"

Seamus knew I baked when I was stressed. I should have hidden the evidence.

"It's just the case that's getting to me." My lie didn't sound right coming out of my mouth, but Seamus seemed to buy it.

"Didn't Molly call yeh?"

I almost dropped the piping bag of pink frosting I was using to create roses for the top of the three-tiered white cake. "No. Did she call you? What did she say?"

"They confirmed the blood was from Claudine's nose," Seamus said. "The case is closed."

"But what about at the hospital? It seemed like someone was still trying to kill Claudine."

"That's the other part Molly wanted to tell me—I'm guessing she didn't call you because she thought you'd be resting."

"Go on," I said. "What's the other part?"

"They arrested Margaret. She has some connections with the dead woman's family. They've done some work for her in the past."

"Illegal work?" I asked.

"Molly didn't go into details."

It was a win. So why didn't it feel like a win?

Seamus wrapped an arm around my shoulders and squeezed. "Stop worryin' so much. Molly has it under control. Leave the rest to her so yeh can rest up."

I finished the pink rose and transferred it onto the cake.

"That's a beautiful cake," Seamus said. "Are you practicing for the wedding?"

The cake was the only thing I hadn't decided on for the wedding. Everything else was planned. "It doesn't seem logical that I'd do my own wedding cake, does it?"

"Does it have to be logical?"

"I guess not," I said.

"Good, because I love yer cakes. They're the best in the world. And I've had my fair share of cakes."

I could feel the heat rising in my cheeks. "Thanks, babe."

"But I don't want yeh to overdo it," he said. "I'm

worried about yeh. It's not every day someone passes out and hits the floor so hard they get a massive concussion."

"I just need to remember to eat regularly and drink more water," I said. And stop randomly finding out about children whose father was my fiancé.

A knock at the door had me nearly sprinting to open it.

"Whoa, whoa," Seamus said with a laugh. "It looks like yer feeling better."

I opened the door to find a tall woman with short spikey black hair, a freckled nose, and bright blue eyes. "Are you Shayla?" She glanced behind her as if someone might be following her.

"I am. Are you Telly?"

"Yes," she said. "May I come in?"

I opened the door wider. "Would you like a slice of cake?"

"No thanks. I'm just here to deliver—" She glanced at Seamus, then back at me. "—the videos you requested."

She held out an unassuming flash drive.

"Let me get you your money," I said.

My purse hung in the closet behind the entry door. I dug in, pulled out a five hundred euro note, and handed it to Telly.

Even though she was trying to play it cool, the widening of her eyes told me everything I needed to know.

"I might have more jobs for you in the future," I said.

"Anything," she said. "I'm pretty good with computers."

"Do you need a ride home?" I asked, looking behind her where no extra car sat in the driveway.

"I rode my bike," she said. "But thanks."

I examined the flash drive in my hand.

"If you want to have a look before I leave with your money, that's fine."

I smiled up at her. "I trust you."

My statement seemed to surprise her more than the handful of cash she'd recently acquired.

"Are you sure about the cake?" I asked. "I can put on some coffee or tea to go with it."

"I really shouldn't," she said. "But thanks."

She turned and walked out the door without looking back.

23

"What's that?" Seamus asked after I'd closed the door. "Who was she?"

"That was Telly—a hacker of sorts. She got access to the hospital cameras for me."

Seamus' eyes widened. "She could get into a lot of trouble doing that."

"I think she's well aware of the trouble she could get in," I said. "But I think she needs the money more."

"Molly already has someone in custody."

"I asked her to get me this before I knew Molly had arrested Margaret." I popped the drive into my laptop and clicked on the icon to open the files. "Do you want to watch with me?"

Seamus groaned but sat down on the couch next to me. "Course I do."

The timestamp was right around when Seamus and I had arrived at the hospital the day before. I wanted to see if Patricia was telling the truth about going to the bathroom and coming back to find Margaret in Claudine's room.

We only had to watch a few minutes before we saw ourselves leave with Roland. About twenty minutes later, Patricia left, presumably heading to the bathroom.

When the doorway was open, the camera peered directly inside the room, where you could see the end of Claudine's bed, her blanket-covered feet, and the monitor that showed her vitals.

After about thirty seconds, Margaret walked into the room, just like Patricia had said. She left the door open—probably to make a quick escape—and walked directly over to the monitors.

From a distance, it was impossible to tell for sure whether she'd turned the sound off, but that's sure what it looked like.

Patricia came back into view of the camera, and my insides tightened. Margaret was caught.

Patricia's body language seemed angry when she caught a startled-looking Margaret. She quickly closed the door, ending the show.

Within twenty more minutes, we were back in the room as they fought.

"This is probably the evidence Molly used to arrest her," Seamus said.

We watched as Roland, Seamus, and I walked into the room, and chaos erupted. Everything seemed so much quicker on video than it had in person.

The recording ended right after the nurses had ordered us all out of the room to take care of Claudine.

"What are the other files?" Seamus asked, pointing to two other video files on the drive.

I clicked on one, which was just another angle of the same footage. "She was definitely thorough."

I was about to close the laptop when something caught my eye in the frame's corner. I pulled the screen closer to me to get a better look.

"What is it?" Seamus asked.

"I think that's the man who drives the junky car," I said, pushing play to see what he did in the video. "This is the parking lot the day Claudine was pushed and the one who followed our car back into town until we started making evasive turns."

Seamus' eyes widened. "Yeh never told me yeh were being followed."

"I forgot until now. What do you think he's doing there?" In the video, he seemed to be almost frozen on the spot. People walked past him as if he wasn't even there.

"Maybe he's the private investigator Margaret hired to follow Claudine and Roland around."

"Sure, but why was he at the castle the same day I was? Roland and Claudine weren't there."

"There's only one way to find out," Seamus said. "We need to talk to him."

"If we can find him." I closed the laptop and sighed.

"Maybe he'll find us." Seamus glanced over at the kitchen. "For now, let's have cake."

"I'll slice you a piece," I said, standing from the couch. "What about you?"

"I'm not hungry," I said. "You know how I am—I bake the things but don't eat the things."

I dished him up a large piece complete with an icing rose and poured a large glass of milk to go along with it.

"You spoil me," Seamus said, digging into the cake.

"I'm going to lie back down for a bit," I said.

Seamus nearly dumped his cake on the floor, trying to stand up and help me.

"I'm fine," I said. "Just tired. It's really okay. Finish your cake."

He eyed me skeptically but nodded in agreement. "I'll check on you soon."

I must have fallen asleep more quickly than I expected because when I woke, it was dark outside, and Seamus hadn't come in to check on me. At least, not that I remembered.

I switched on the lamp next to the bed and tiptoed to the living room, expecting to find Seamus asleep on the couch. Instead, I found his half-eaten piece of cake, a full glass of warm milk, and a hastily scribbled note.

Shay - had to run to the stables. Be back soon.

He had to have written it just as I'd drifted off to sleep hours ago.

Panic overcame me. What if something had happened to one of the horses? What if something had happened to Cupid?

I pulled on my boots and jacket and hurried outside.

Seamus had taken our fancy golf cart, so I got in the car and drove it up the road to the stables.

Seamus, Gráinne, Donal, and several of the stable staff stood outside the big barn in a circle.

The minute Seamus turned to look at who was coming up the drive, I knew something was wrong.

I hopped out of the car and hurried over. Seamus buried his head into my shoulder as a muted sob burst from his lips.

When I looked at the others, they seemed to have been crying too. "What happened?" My voice sounded far away.

"One of the mares died," Gráinne said, her voice gravely with emotion. "She was giving birth and lost too much blood."

"And the foal?" I asked.

"The vet's in with her right now, but it's not looking good," Gráinne said.

Seamus stood and looked at me with his sad eyes. "I need a drink. Let's go to the pub."

I glanced at Gráinne, who nodded in approval. Not that we had to have her approval to go out, I just didn't know if leaving in the middle of the ordeal was the best idea.

I drove into town as Seamus tried to compose himself.

Once at the pub, I parked as close as possible, which was still a couple of blocks away, and we walked hand in hand to the crowded bar.

Seamus and I found an empty—but dirty—high-top table in the back. There were no chairs around the high-top tables, which allowed more people to crowd into the overstuffed pub. It was amazing they didn't get in trouble with the fire marshal.

Loud music and even louder conversations made it impossible to hear anything Seamus was saying—that is if he'd been saying anything. He didn't seem much in the mood for talking tonight.

Harry—the owner of the pub—dropped off two Guinness at our table without saying much. It was our regular order, and we had a running tab that just magically got paid. Probably by Gráinne.

Seamus took a hearty drink before slipping his glass back onto the table.

I reached across and squeezed his hand, taking a sip of my beer.

"If it isn't Shayla Murphy, the gold digger herself," a man shouted directly behind me.

I turned to find a man with a ponytail and a mean grin on his face staring at me.

Seamus was at my side within seconds. "Who are you?"

"My name doesn't matter," the man said. "It's my message I want you to hear." He dropped his beer on the table next to ours and put his hands in the air before shouting for everyone to quiet down.

Eventually, the pub's noise level lowered to a dull roar as people craned their necks to see what was happening.

The man shouted, "The Anti Shayla Brigade is here in full force tonight, and we demand Shayla Murphy return to America where she belongs and leave our beloved O'Malley alone."

Several people in the pub cheered. A couple booed.

The dull roar lowered to a chirp.

"That's it?" Seamus said. "Yeh have to be kidding, right?"

"I am not kidding in the slightest," the man with the ponytail said. "We are prepared to do whatever it takes to return Shayla to America."

"You will not touch a hair on her head," Seamus said. "She's the love of me life, and I'm going to marry her no matter what yeh lot say about it."

"So be it," the man said. "You've not heard the last of the ASB!"

He took his drink off the table and tipped it back, chugging it down.

When the glass was empty, he slammed it back on the table and wiped the foam off his lips just before he fell to the ground dead.

24

W hen the crowd realized what had happened, people started screaming and pushing their way out of the pub.

"Slow down, slow down," Harry said. "Don't be trampling each other."

Seamus called the Gardaí to report the man's collapse as I reached down to check for a pulse.

Nothing.

A fast-acting poison was the only thing that made sense. And with him being in the ASB, I was confident I would take the blame.

I started compressions to keep his heart pumping. I couldn't do rescue breaths because of the possibility of poison.

Ponytail man didn't seem to be getting any better with the compressions, but the medics arrived shortly and took over. Right behind them, Molly rushed in, holding her badge as if we didn't all know she was a garda.

"What happened?" She surveyed the scene. The pub

was nearly empty minus the medics, ponytail man, Seamus, the gardaí, Harry, and me. The high-top tables were littered with abandoned plates of food, spilled drinks, and various personal effects.

"He was part of the Anti-Shayla Brigade," I said, unable to look at her, fearing I'd somehow give away her secret. "I think he was trying to threaten or scare me into returning to America. Then he chugged his beer and almost instantly fell to the ground dead. He didn't have a pulse, so I started compressions."

Seamus glanced at the high-top table we'd been standing by. "Shay, yeh got a Guinness, right?"

"As always," I said.

"Did yeh drink any of it?" Seamus asked.

I turned to see what he was talking about to find a beer on our table that wasn't mine. Mine was missing.

"I had a sip when Harry dropped it off." I looked down at the glass on the ground next to ponytail guy, realization striking me square in the chest. "The poison was meant for me."

"What do yeh mean the poison was meant for you?" Molly asked.

"He drank my beer on accident," I said, picking up the extra glass on our table. "This was his. I don't know what it is, but it's not Guinness."

"And yer certain yeh took a sip of it when it reached the table?" Molly asked.

I nodded. "One hundred percent."

"Are yeh feeling all right?" Seamus asked, worry overtaking his features. "I knew it was a bad idea to come to the pub to drown my sorrow. We should have stayed home."

I put a hand on his arm. "Shh, it's okay. I'm fine. Whoever slipped poison in my drink did it after it had been delivered to the table. Probably while he was making his speech."

"Do yeh think he was in on it?" Seamus asked. "Like as a decoy?"

"If someone made him a decoy, they must not have told him their plan," Molly said. "Otherwise, I suspect he'd have been more careful about which beer he drank."

A wave of dread came over me. "Do you think the woman you found over the cliff could have been part of the ASB? Maybe she'd been aiming to push me off the balcony after all."

"Let's take a breath," Molly said. "Though that might be the case, there is also the possibility that the two victims were somehow related. We have to rule that out as well."

"They're related all right," Harry said. "That's Claudine's brother—Kellen."

"Wait, the man with the ponytail—the one who just fell dead—is Claudine's brother?" I gaped at Harry. "As in the Claudine who is fighting for her life in the hospital as we speak?"

"Yep," Harry said.

"Grand," Molly said. "I suppose that means we either have someone who keeps trying to kill you or someone who has it out for Claudine's family."

"Do you think Margaret had something to do with this

one too?" Seamus asked. "I'm sure she could pull strings even from lockup."

"No way of telling yet," Molly said, sucking in a deep breath. "I best be getting onto processing this crime scene. You know the drill. If yeh think of anything else that might be important, let me know."

Seamus nodded and led me out of the pub.

When we slipped into the car, my phone dinged in my purse with a text message.

It's Telly—I can help solve this with you.

I smiled at her initiative.

"What's that smile for?" Seamus asked.

I stopped smiling. "Sorry, wrong time for that. I just got this text message from Telly."

"Yeh can smile any time," Seamus said. "She seems eager for the work. Are yeh gonna let her help?"

"I don't know what she'd do."

"Ask her."

Good idea. I typed out a quick message.

what do you think you'll be able to help me with

The three dots instantly started moving to indicate Telly was responding.

I can hack into anything. No one in town knows me. And even if they do, I can make myself invisible.

I wasn't sure how a woman of her height and beauty

would make herself invisible, but the hacking could come in handy.

"Is there anything you can think of that we need hacked?"

Seamus shrugged.

My brain was trying to grasp details when another message came in.

We can start by taking down the ASB.

"What did she say?" Seamus asked.

I showed him the phone.

A smile washed over his face. "Perfect."

deal my house tomorrow morning

Eight o'clock work for you?

perfect

I slid the phone back into my purse and looked out the window. We were stopped at a stop sign with the pub to my left. Seamus waited as the medics wheeled Kellen's sheet-covered body out of the pub and into the ambulance.

A bright pink car honked, swerved around us, and nearly crashed into the front of the ambulance. It had barely squealed to a stop when Patricia flung the door open and rushed to the medics.

She must have known one of them because when he nodded, she let out a gut-wrenching scream before doubling over and vomiting all over the ground.

The medic patted her on the back, uncertainty in his eyes.

Part of me wanted to get out and help somehow—to hug Patricia or something. Then I remembered what she said about not liking me. I'd only make it worse if I showed up right now.

"Let's go home," I said to Seamus.

He nodded and started down the road.

"Wait," I said. "There it is. The junky car."

I pointed in the opposite direction.

Seamus made a U-turn so quickly that the tires squealed. "I think it's time we had a chat with him."

25

Seamus navigated the streets like a professional driver. The guy in the junky car had no chance once we caught up to him.

Unfortunately, with all the people leaving the pub at the same time, catching him proved to be a tricky task.

"He went down there," I said, pointing down a narrow lane lined on both sides by stone walls.

Seamus took the tight turn at full speed, knocking one of the mirrors off the side of the car. "Happens all the time. It's no big deal."

I almost laughed at the hilarity of it. No big deal to knock a mirror off was something a rich person would say. And Seamus was rich. It still boggled my mind to think about it.

"Do you think Patricia is part of the ASB?" I asked. "She's made it very apparent she doesn't like me."

"Yeh can dislike someone and not want to cause their death."

"I guess all that talk about the ASB being a peaceful organization wasn't exactly true, was it?"

Seamus took another turn, this time slower. The junky car's taillights were getting brighter as we gained on him.

"Maybe some are, and some aren't," Seamus said. "Without a true leader, there might not be a set of rules."

"Telly will figure it out."

"How did you meet Telly again?"

"Claudine's ex-boyfriend's mom recommended her." As the words came out of my mouth, they sounded less and less reliable.

"And you trust her?"

I usually had a pretty good intuition about things and people. "Yeah, I think so."

"How about we make sure there's a guard around when she's there, just in case? At least until people stop trying to kill you."

"I can handle that."

"There, I think we got him." The brake lights on the junky car turned off as the car came to a stop.

Whoever had been driving jumped out and scaled the rock wall, running through a yard into a rather large house. It was too dark to make out whether the person was the man I'd seen in the video, but it only made sense it would be him.

"Shall we go talk to him?" Seamus asked, pulling his car behind the junky one.

I got out and peeked inside the car. Several pizza boxes, a couple of manila envelopes, candy wrappers, and soda bottles littered the seats and the floor. "Not the cleanest person in the world." I snapped a couple of photos of the inside of the car and one of the license plates.

"Probably long nights of watching Roland and Claudine go in and out of clubs," Seamus said.

We used the gate and walked up the stone walkway to the house the person had gone inside.

Seamus knocked on the door with enough force to nearly break the knocker.

"How about I do the talking?" I said.

Seamus nodded. He'd been through a lot tonight, and I was afraid his emotions might get the better of him.

When no one answered, I knocked again with slightly less force.

The door opened to a man who looked to be in his sixties with a well-groomed gray beard, slightly damp gray hair, and bright green eyes, wearing a knee-length robe with plaid pajamas underneath. He held a pipe in his hand and a confused expression on his face. "Can I help yeh with something?"

Through the small sliver in the door, his house looked well-furnished and expensive, and the hum of music drifted to my ears. "Uh, did someone just run into your house?" The words felt ridiculous coming out of my mouth.

"Run into my house?" the man said. "As in with their car?"

"Er, no," I said. "As in, opened your door and ran inside?"

"The door was locked," he said. "Maybe you're mistaking my house for another."

"Does anyone else live here?" Seamus asked.

"Since me wife passed, it's just me."

"I know this seems strange," I said. "But you could be in danger. Were you in the shower just before you opened the door?"

"What an intrusive question," he said. "I suppose it's what I should expect from an American, but still."

"I only ask because if someone ran inside when you couldn't hear them and they're still inside, they could hurt you."

He huffed. "I assure yeh no one is in me home but me. Me doors were locked, me security system set, and I'd been out of the shower for over a half hour. Now, if yer finished botherin' me, I suggest you leave so I don't have to call the Gardaí."

Seamus gently grabbed me by the crook of the arm when he noticed my hesitation. "We're so sorry to bother yeh."

"Is that your car?" I asked, pointing to the junker. "Or do you know whose it is?"

The man squinted. "Me cars stay in the garage where they belong. I've never seen that car in me life."

He shut the door in our faces.

"That went well," Seamus said as we walked back to our car.

"Let's pretend like we're leaving and see if he comes back out. Maybe that was just a disguise or something."

"Or maybe we saw wrong," Seamus said. "It's dark. Maybe whoever was driving the car ran through the garden and hid somewhere beyond the house."

"Can we just wait and watch for a few minutes?"

Seamus smiled. "Of course, love."

We waited for more than a few minutes. After at least an hour, I gave up hope of catching whoever had driven the car.

"I'm sure we'll see him again," Seamus said. "Especially since it seems like he's following you now."

The thought of someone following me at the same time someone seemed to want me dead was enough to make my stomach turn.

A chime emitted from the car speakers. Seamus pressed a button to answer the call. "Hello?"

"Hello, it's me," Gráinne said. "The filly is stable. She's a fighter just like her mam."

Seamus clenched a celebratory fist. "That's wonderful news."

"I think she may be one of the best fillies we've ever bred."

"We'll come to visit her when we get back." Seamus glanced at me for approval.

I nodded so hard it felt like my head might pop off my shoulders. I loved seeing the newborn foals.

"I'm sure Wes will be happy to see you."

Wes was in charge of the stables. He was the boss of the other stable staff and kept things running as smoothly as cake frosting through a brand-new piping bag and fresh tip.

We found Wes in the dimly lit barn with the filly asleep on his lap.

I did my best not to squeal and wake her up. She was precious.

"She's taken two bottles," Wes said.

Seamus nodded and bent down to look at her face. "I've never seen such an interesting marking."

She had a white face while her body—all the way up past her ears—was a dark brown. Her legs also had touches of white here and there, while her mane and tail were almost black.

"You can pet her," Seamus said to me.

I sat against the stall wall next to Wes and slid a hand down the side of her neck from her ear to her shoulder.

She lifted her head and looked at me, her nostrils opening slightly wider to take in my scent, before lowering her head back down onto my legs, allowing Wes to stand.

"I'm too old to be sitting on the ground like that," he said with a smile.

I continued to rub her neck and scratch behind her ears. If possible, I'd stay in that stall with her forever.

Magella prepared a few breakfast items and delicious lattes for my meeting with Telly.

Seamus had offered to stay, but after last night he'd also hired a private security company to watch over the property just in case whoever was attacking people was trying to murder me.

At five minutes to eight, a knock sounded at the door.

The woman in the security uniform assured me Telly had been patted down and was clear to come in.

"That's new," Telly said when the door was closed.

"Last night, I was almost poisoned," I said. "Seamus is convinced someone is out to kill me."

"He's not the only one." Telly had her black hair even more spiked than the day before. Today, her eyes were hazel green.

"You too? Or someone you know?"

She laughed. "I don't know anyone."

"Except me."

She quirked an eyebrow but didn't say anything about how we actually didn't know each other at all. "Last night at the pub, someone slipped poison into your drink."

"Yes," I said. "That's the conclusion I came to as well."

She shook her head. "I'm not hypothesizing. I'm stating facts. I saw someone put poison in your drink."

"Why didn't you tell me? I could have been the one in the morgue this morning."

"I wasn't physically there."

"Then how'd you—"

"Don't ask." She held a hand up, revealing what looked like an old circular burn scar on her palm. "It happened too quickly. The guy started making a fuss, and the person —I couldn't identify them—popped up almost out of nowhere. They used a syringe without the needle to push something—the poison—into your drink. I was about to call your phone, but then the guy with the ponytail took it and downed it."

I thought this through, trying to make it make sense in my mind. "But there aren't any cameras in the pub. Harry wouldn't allow it."

"I don't need CCTV cameras to access video footage. Do you realize how many people were at the pub last night? How many people wanted to get ponytail's speech on video?"

"You made it sound like you hacked your way into something to get the footage."

She shrugged. "Why break laws when the footage is out there for everyone to see?"

Telly pulled the laptop from her bag and set it on the table while taking a piece of bacon and nibbling on it like a rabbit. When the screen flickered on, she hit a few keys and pulled up a video from social media showing a person dressed in all black approaching my table, squirting something into my drink, and hurrying away just before Kellen picked the glass up and chugged it down.

"Did you see it?" Telly asked.

"See what?"

She rewound the video and played it more slowly. The hooded figure was unrecognizable, but something on their shirt gave them away. "The pin."

"Very good." Telly seemed impressed. "It's an ASB pin —see?" She zoomed in on the still shot of the video, causing it to blur, but the letters ASB were easy to pick out, even on a pixelated image.

"I guess that settles it," I said. "They're trying to kill me."

"It does seem that way," she said. "At least in this instance."

"Do you have a way to pull footage from the Ballywick Castle surveillance when Claudine was pushed?"

She shook her head. "Already tried. The system was offline all day."

"Intentionally?"

"No way to know," she said. "Is there any possibility that these two instances weren't connected?"

"In my professional opinion, as a police officer, it's more likely that they are connected than not."

"You're a police officer?" Telly looked like a deer caught in the headlights, unsure where to run to avoid danger. "Like an American police officer?"

"I used to be."

Telly shut her laptop and shoved it back in her bag. "This was a bad idea. I'm sorry to have wasted your time."

Before I could say anything else, she was out the door and riding off down the driveway on her bicycle.

"What was that about?" the security woman guarding the cottage asked.

I shrugged. There was no reason to tell her that Telly freaked out when she found out I used to be a police officer. "I think she forgot an appointment or something. Did you do a background check on her before she came over?"

"We tried," the woman said. "But nothing came up. We don't have access to international records, so it's probably because she's new in town and hasn't yet been entered into our system."

"Thanks," I said. "Would you like a coffee or some bacon? They're fresh, and there's no way I'll be able to eat it all."

She glanced out toward the driveway as if she may have been being watched. "I probably shouldn't."

"I can bring it out here to you," I said. "Then you don't have to leave your post."

She hemmed and hawed a bit and then finally gave in. "Okay, but just one piece of bacon and a black coffee. You can put it in my travel mug if that's all right?"

She handed me the travel mug. I quickly rinsed it, filled it with the coffee, and picked up a few pieces of bacon with a napkin.

"I got you a few pieces in case you decide you want more. If you don't, just toss it in the garbage."

She smiled and sipped the coffee. "Thank you."

"Any time."

I started to turn back into the house when she asked, "Are you afraid?"

"Afraid of what?"

"The people who may or may not be trying to kill you?"

I looked out over the green of the hillsides surrounding us, the fog barely lifting into the sky. "Not really. I probably should be, but my thoughts are more focused on trying to find out who's behind this."

"Good luck with that," she said. "And thanks for the coffee and bacon."

I closed the door and grabbed my laptop. I might not have been as savvy with a computer as a hacker, but I knew my way around social media. Maybe I could find a video from a different angle that gave away some of the person's face.

The sheer number of videos from that night overwhelmed me. Especially how many had the hashtag ASB. Were there that many people around Ballywick who didn't want me to marry Seamus?

Most of the footage was taken of Kellen's dramatic speech and drink, resulting in his death. Not many had been shot from behind him.

At least not many that were at the top of the page. I saw different angles as I scrolled down to the less-liked and less-viewed videos. Ones that didn't show Kellen falling in a heap. Some didn't even show his face, and his words were so muffled it could have been anyone speaking.

It was in one of those videos that I caught a break.

None of the videos showed a good view of the person's face, but one got a closeup of the person's hand . . . complete with bright pink fingernail polish.

There was only one person I could think of who would wear such a bright shade of pink —Patricia.

Her entire essence was pink. Even her car was pink.

If anyone had been wearing pink nail polish, it would have been her.

I dialed Molly's number and waited for her to answer.

"I know, I know, I'm gonna tell him," Molly said. "I just haven't had a chance with everything on this case."

"That's not why I'm calling. I know who did it."

"You know who did what?"

"I know who tried to poison me."

The other end of the line was silent for five seconds before Molly said, "What're yeh waiting for? Give it a lash."

"It was Patricia," I said.

"Do yeh have evidence?"

"A bit," I said, my resolve fading. The only evidence I

had was the color pink. How many other women in the country liked pink? Probably a lot. Molly was going to laugh at me the moment I told her my theory.

"Come on. I don't have all day."

"I went through the social media videos from last night—mostly ones taken by members of the ASB—and one zoomed in on the person's hand as they slipped the syringe of poison into my glass. That person was wearing pink nail polish."

"And you've recently seen Patricia with pink nail polish on her fingernails?"

"Well, I—"

"That's a no." Molly sighed. "I know Patricia likes the color pink, but so do a lot of people—men included. It could have been anyone with pink nails."

Her mention of men reminded me of the guy in the junky car. Could he have been wearing pink polish?

"You could check in on her and see," I said. "If she's wearing pink polish, ask her a few questions. What can it hurt?"

"Other than the poison, there's zero evidence in last night's incident. We're fairly certain we found who's responsible for Claudine's attempted murder, but being as though the suspect is dead, it's hard to prove anything."

"But you know she was connected to Margaret."

"Barely," Molly said. "She's connected to practically everyone in Ireland."

"She turned off Claudine's monitors in the hospital, though."

Crap.

I wasn't supposed to say that. She didn't know that I'd had access to the video footage.

"How did you know about Margaret turning off the monitor?"

I didn't want to lie to her, but I couldn't tell her I'd hired someone to hack into the system. "I can't tell you that."

"Is there anything else yeh know that I should know?"

I considered this for a moment. "Only the pink polish."

She sighed. "I'll need more than pink polish to close this case. Especially now that Margaret has been released."

"Released?" I asked. "But why? She did turn the machine off."

"She turned the beeping off because it reminded her of the last time she was in the hospital, which was a bad experience for her. Plus, she was still in custody last night when Kellen was poisoned."

"Couldn't she have had someone else do that as she would have for Claudine?"

"That's just the thing," Molly said. "We had all of her known associates at the station last night. Every single one. She hasn't lied about her travel plans. She hasn't made any large withdrawals or transfers. There is no evidence that she has anything to do with these crimes."

I could hear the exhaustion in Molly's voice.

"There's one associate you didn't have in custody last night," I said. "He drives a junky car and has been tailing me. I think he's a PI."

"I'm well aware of this PI. He's annoying but not a murderer."

"How's your daughter?" I asked, giving up on discussing the case. "Is her finger okay?"

"It'll be fine," she said. "Thankfully, she can still go to school with it. I don't know what I would have done if she had to stay home."

My mind instantly went to the thought that she could come over and hang out with me. I quickly pushed it away as that was way too sticky a situation for me to walk into. "That's good. I'm glad she's okay."

"I will tell him," Molly said. "Soon. I promise. Before the end of the week."

"I believe you."

We hung up, and within seconds my phone rang again.

It was my mother.

I sucked in a breath and answered. "Hi, Mom."

"Shayla? Can you hear me?" she practically screamed into the phone.

"I can hear you," I said. "Just because we're far away distance-wise doesn't mean the phones don't work the same."

"I swear, they're less reliable over oceans."

"How's the wedding planning?" I asked, trying to change the subject.

"It's wonderful," she said, a dreamy note in her voice. "I just got my dress. I think you'd love it."

"Can you send me a picture?"

"I couldn't do that. It'll just have to be a surprise. If you wanted to see it so badly, you should've been here when I was trying them on."

"I didn't know you had plans to try on dresses, or I might have been able to visit."

"That would be a silly reason to travel all that way. It's just a wedding dress."

Her circular reasoning always frustrated me. But unlike teenage me, adult me knew how to keep her feelings to herself. "I haven't even looked for a dress. It's been a crazy week."

"How's the case going?" she asked, seemingly more excited about this subject than wedding dresses. "Did you find any scorned ex-lovers?"

"There was a lead with one, but that fell through. He's been in America since he got out of jail."

"Want me to run his name and confirm that?"

She technically wasn't a police officer anymore, but she still had her way of staying in the loop and accessing the systems.

"Nah, it's okay. I think Molly already did."

"Is that the same Molly Seamus dated when he lived here?"

"Yep." I didn't want to get into this discussion again. My mom was more than a little bit territorial when it came to men. "She's a good officer. I'm sure she can handle it. Plus, they think they know who pushed her over the balcony. That person is dead now, though."

"Maybe that person was murdered by the person who really did it," Mom said.

I guess I'd just assumed the woman in white with the snake tattoo had jumped after she'd pushed Claudine— probably because if Claudine woke up, she'd be able to identify her. "There was blood on her pants consistent with what would have happened when Claudine fell over the rail and hit her nose. It's a pretty sure thing that she did it."

"Did she leave a note? Did she seem suicidal? Have they even asked these questions?"

I didn't know if Molly had asked anyone those questions, but I knew I hadn't.

"Why else would someone want to kill her?"

"Maybe someone saw her do it and wanted revenge."

There were only two people I could think of who would care enough about Claudine to kill the person who tried to kill her—Patricia and Roland. Claudine's brother hadn't even been to her hospital room to visit.

"Thanks for the help," I said. "Those are good ideas."

"I miss you, kid."

I nearly dropped the phone. She'd hardly ever said she missed me. Even when I went to camp for two months over the summer in high school, she'd never said she missed me.

"I miss you too," I said. "Thanks for calling."

"You know, the phone works both ways. You can call me whenever you want or need some help with the case."

"I know, I'm sorry," I said. "I'm not great at keeping in touch lately."

I thought about how I hadn't called Rylie in what felt like forever. I made a mental note to shoot her a text to see how life was going.

"I have to go now," she said. "I'll talk to you soon. Tell your future *in-laws* I say hello and that I can't wait to meet them at the wedding in *June*."

"Will do," I said. "Bye."

She hung up without another word.

I sighed and sat back on the couch. When I became a mom, I'd never hang up on my children without telling them how much I loved them.

I made a few calls to the hospital and Ballywick Castle and was informed that Roland was out of town on business and Patricia was in the middle of a wedding.

I called for the car service, swiped on a couple of coats of mascara, tied my curls back into a nice bun, and threw on a nicer dress so I would fit in with the wedding. This was not the time to stand out.

All I needed to do was go in, see Patricia's fingernails, and leave. If her nails were pink, I'd report it to Molly, and she could take it from there. If they weren't pink, I'd need to figure out if they had been pink the night before.

The driver was friendly, though overprotective. He tried to insist on going inside the castle with me, but I assured him there were plenty of people around for the wedding and that if Patricia were the one trying to kill me, it wouldn't make sense for her to do so with so many witnesses.

He opened the door and stood next to the car. "If I so much as hear a scream, I'm coming in."

I nodded.

If he heard a scream, it would probably be too late, though I didn't tell him that.

One of the side doors was open, so I snuck in to avoid the actual wedding guests. As the view opened to the center of the castle, my breath caught in my chest.

The wedding was set up almost identical to how I pictured ours. Rows of white chairs with a long aisle down the center led to a raised platform and a gorgeous wooden arch.

Tears stung my eyes. In only a couple of months, I would walk down this same aisle toward Seamus. I watched the couple as they met on the stage and stared in a trance as the wedding official spoke to them and their guests.

It wasn't until they were pronounced husband and wife, kissed, and turned to the audience that I recognized them as the couple I'd passed the day Patricia wanted me to sign that updated contract. The couple who had only just gotten engaged.

How had they gotten such a quick wedding date if the venue was completely booked?

Then another realization hit me.

Margaret said she'd had the ring in her purse only three weeks ago, which meant Roland and Claudine had gotten engaged after we had. They'd requested the date after we had.

"What are you doing here?" Patricia hissed from behind me.

I turned, anger flowing through my veins. "You lied to me. I can prove you lied to me."

She shook her head. "You can prove nothing."

"You told us that Claudine and Roland had requested the date before we had, but that's categorically impossible since they got engaged after us. You told me there were no other openings until November. Yet, this couple only just visited the castle for the first time, and here they are getting married less than a week later."

"Get over yourself," she said. "You are not the most important person in the world. You're a nobody. I don't know what Seamus sees in you."

"Someone who's not after his money, I suppose."

"Like that's true," she said.

"I didn't even know he was rich. I thought he was just a park ranger whose family lived in some little house in Ireland."

"It's preposterous to think you didn't know who Seamus O'Malley is."

I shrugged. "You can think whatever you want."

"Why are you here? Who cares if I lied, you got the date you wanted, didn't you?"

"I wanted to ask you about your assistant—the one who died."

Several people turned to look at me when I mentioned death.

"Let's go to my office and discuss it." Patricia walked away, her heels clicking loudly on the stone.

Once we were in and she'd closed the door, she said, "I have already discussed everything I know about my assistant with the gardaí officers. She was withdrawn and had just gone through a nasty breakup. My guess is she was jealous of Claudine and pushed her then jumped out of guilt."

"Did she leave a note?"

"A note?"

"Like a suicide note?"

"Not that I know of."

"Did she have family around here?"

"Just the ex-boyfriend," Patricia said. "Her family lives up north."

"Have you spoken with them?"

Patricia sighed. "I assumed the gardaí would be doing that."

"Are you part of the Anti-Shayla Brigade?"

"The what?" Patricia's eyes darted to the door.

"I'm certain you know what it is. Kellen was part of it."

"Don't you ever speak his name again." She balled her fists at her sides.

"Was your assistant part of the ASB?"

"If she was, I was unaware."

"Do you think she tried to kill me but got Claudine instead?"

"The ASB is a peaceful group," Patricia said, tears welling in her eyes. "The only thing bad about it was how much time it took away from my time with Kellen. He put everything into that stupid club."

"If it was so peaceful, why did he say the ASB would get rid of me in any way possible?"

"It was a figure of speech. He would never have hurt anyone."

"Maybe not him directly, but maybe there are some rogue ASB members. And maybe he was talking to them."

Patricia shrugged. "I wouldn't know."

A knock at the door interrupted us, and Anna—the assistant who had tried to get me to sign the new contract—stepped inside.

Patricia motioned for her to come closer.

She glanced at me and then quickly away before hurrying to Patricia's side.

Patricia yanked the other woman's hand toward her and wrote something on it in black marker.

I studied both of their nails. Patricia's were free of all polish.

"I like your nails," I said to the assistant, whose dark blue nails looked freshly manicured. "Where did you get them done?"

"In town," she said. "At Ballywick Nails. Talk to Jenna. She's the best."

"Thanks," I said.

She glanced down at her hand, nodded once, and quickly left the room.

"Now, if there's nothing else, I have a wedding I need to return to."

I went back out the side door where I'd come in. Before I could take a step, someone was behind me with their hand clasped over my mouth.

"Don't scream." He was strong, but I was trained for this exact situation.

I grabbed his wrist and yanked his hand off my mouth.

As I sucked in a breath to scream, he said in a deep Irish accent, "I have information about yer case."

I whipped around to face him, my gaze going straight to his bright green eyes. The same eyes I'd seen the night before. Only this time, the man didn't have a gray beard and hair. Now, he had bright red hair and a clean-shaven face.

I glared at him. "You tried to poison me last night, didn't you?"

This seemed to catch him completely off guard.

"Don't play dumb," I said. "You've been following me. I've seen you in your junky old car."

"'Tis me job to follow. Not to kill."

"Who hired you?"

"That's none of yer business." He took a step away from me. "Look, if yeh don't be wantin' the information about yer case, I'll be takin' me leave."

"What do you think you know?"

A smile broached his lips. Without the beard, he was actually rather cute—very Irish. "Did yeh check the camera footage?"

"Which camera footage?"

"The castle cameras."

"The system was out the day Claudine fell," I said. "Whether that was intentional or not, I wouldn't know."

"Not the entire system."

"Can you just tell me what you're getting at? I have places to be."

"There are two sets of camera systems on the property

—the ones that keep the castle secure and the ones that keep the staff in check."

I shifted from one foot to the other, trying not to give away my excitement. "How do you know this?"

"It's me job to know," he said. "Check the staff cameras. They might show something you missed."

He turned to walk away. I hurried to catch up.

"You were there that day," I said. "What did you see?"

"I'm not at liberty to discuss me observations that day. It's in me contract."

He had to be the PI that Margaret had hired. "Why are you telling me all this? Why not go to the Gardaí?"

"The Gardaí and I don't exactly see eye to eye," he said. "Plus, you're making quite a name for yourself here."

I was? As what, the nosy American?

"I must crack on now. I've lots to do. It's probably best we're not seen together." He picked up his pace toward the parking lot and his junky car.

"What's your name?" I asked.

He turned back and looked at me. "Finn—me name's Finn."

"Nice to meet you, Finn," I said.

"Yeh sure 'bout that?" He laughed and slipped into the front seat of his car, leaving me with more questions than I could verbalize.

29

As much as I wanted to check the security cameras, I didn't have that skill set, and I was reasonably certain Patricia wouldn't give me access.

Before I went to Molly with more useless information, I figured I'd try Telly.

hey, sorry about last night. im not a police officer anymore. whatever you think I'm going to do, i won't. i have no intentions of digging into your past. but i do need your help. apparently there are two different camera systems at the castle. the one watching the staff may not have been turned off that day. i'll pay you double what i paid last time

I hit the send button and hoped for the best. I'd already asked my driver slash security guard to take me to the nail salon before we headed home. As we headed back into town, I searched on my phone for the Anti-Shayla Brigade's website. The first page had a letter written to

Kellen with a video of his last speech in the pub. It cut off right before he drank the beer and showed nothing more than the ones online had.

Right below this video was another video titled New Leadership, Same Mission.

I clicked the play button and turned the sound up.

A person appeared on screen in a hood, the shadows concealing their identity.

When the person spoke, it was apparent the voice had been digitally altered to conceal the identity of the new leader.

"It is with great sadness that I take over the position of leadership in the ASB. Our mission remains steadfast—to do anything within our abilities to send Shayla Murphy back to America, leaving our beloved Seamus to marry a proper Irishwoman.

"I implore you do not stoop to Shayla Murphy's level and resort to violence. You may be in danger in her presence, just as Kellen was. We have video evidence that proves she is the one who poisoned the drink and then switched it with his. This evidence has been forwarded to the proper authorities, and we remain hopeful that she will be punished to the full degree for this attack and the one on Kellen's sister, Claudine.

"Shayla is a danger to Seamus and a danger to Ireland. She's brainwashed him into thinking she's what's best for him. We have to make him see the truth about her. Dig up any dirt you can find. Keep sending letters. Stick to your plans. We will prevail. For Claudine. For Seamus. For Kellen. For Ireland."

The video went black.

I sat staring at the blank screen for several long minutes.

The driver cleared his throat. "I'm sorry to eavesdrop, but please do not hold the whole of Ireland accountable for this one terrorist group. Most of us love yeh. These are just the crazies coming out of the woodwork."

My emotions were all over the place. I didn't know whether I was about to cry or throw up.

I turned the phone screen off and slipped it back inside my purse as we pulled up to the nail salon. I steadied my nerves before stepping out of the car.

"Do yeh want me to come inside?" the driver asked with worry in his eyes.

"I'll be okay," I said. "Thank you for your kindness."

He nodded and held the salon door open for me before returning to lean against the car.

"Can I help yeh?" A woman with bright orange hair and probably ten piercings on her face asked.

"I'd like a manicure with Jenna, if possible."

She smiled. "I'm Jenna, and yer in luck. I just freed up."

I followed her back to her table. There were only three manicure stations, and the other two were empty. In fact, we were the only two people in the room.

"How'd yeh hear about me?" Jenna asked as she started pulling out her tools.

"One of the women over at Ballywick Castle told me you're the best," I said. "Her nails were a gorgeous blue."

Jenna nodded. "Do yeh want the same thing?"

"Uh, sure." I hadn't considered how I'd get my nails

done, but that seemed as good a color as any. "How long will they last? It's just hers looked so fresh."

"They'll last a while," Jenna said, not expanding.

She was more tight-lipped than I expected. Weren't manicurists the chatty type? Or was that hair stylists? If I'd done more to keep myself styled, I would know.

I pushed the thought away. Now was not the time to get down on myself. I was here to get answers, and that was what I'd do.

"Would yeh like a free massage while I do yer nails?" Jenna asked, her tone brightening slightly.

A massage sounded incredible with the day I'd had. "That would be wonderful."

She pulled out her phone, sent a text, and within seconds, another woman wheeled out one of those massage chairs you see in the mall.

"Let's just replace that chair you're on," the woman said with a smile.

I stood and then straddled the chair, resting my face on the opening where all I could see was the edge of the manicure table and the floor.

They went to work silently, each of them doing their job.

The massage was harder than I would have liked, but I didn't want to correct her. Surely, she knew better than I did about how to do a back massage. Maybe I just had a lot of kinks or something.

"Do you book up pretty quickly here?" I asked after at least a half hour of silence.

"Sometimes," Jenna said. "It just depends on the day."

Today was Saturday. "Back in the states, I usually got

my nails done on Fridays, but yesterday was so crazy I didn't get into town. Are Fridays usually busy?"

"Not particularly," Jenna said.

"Maybe I can come at the same time as the woman from Ballywick since she and I seem to have the same taste in color. Then you wouldn't have to pull the same nail polish twice."

"It's no bother," Jenna said.

Dang. She wasn't giving me anything.

"That's a nice ring you have," Jenna said. "Who's the lucky guy?"

I hesitated. If they hadn't already recognized me, they probably weren't part of the ASB, but if they were, I could be in danger if I told them.

"He's from America," I said. "We're thinking of settling down in Ballywick."

"It's a grand place to live," Jenna replied. "I've lived here me entire life."

"So have I," the masseuse said. "I was a bit younger in school than Jenna."

"We only became friends when we started working together," Jenna said.

"My best friend and I became friends working together too." I did a mental head slap. I still hadn't texted or called Rylie.

"Is that who yer marryin'?" The masseuse asked.

"No," I said. "Though I met the guy I'm marrying at work too."

"Yer leavin' yer best friend in the states?" Jenna asked, her voice shocked.

"I'm sure we'll visit each other a lot," I said. "And technology is great. We can FaceTime and text whenever."

"Those must have been good jobs in America if yeh can afford to travel internationally so often," Jenna said.

Did I sense a hint of disdain in her voice? Maybe she didn't like Americans. Or maybe she knew who I was and had been faking it all this time.

"Oh, I think I feel my phone vibrating. I should probably—"

The masseuse pushed harder on a tender spot taking my breath away.

"Ooh, that might be a bit too hard," I said, but she didn't let up.

"You have a serious knot in your back. I'm just working it out." The masseuse pushed harder, bringing tears to my eyes.

"I'm sure whoever it is on the phone can wait," Jenna said.

I moved a bit, trying to relieve the pressure from what felt like her knuckles pushing through my muscle and into my ribs.

"Don't move," the masseuse whispered in my ear. "You think we don't know who you are?"

The hairs on the back of my neck stood straight up. I should have seen this coming.

I tried to pull my hands away, but Jenna held them tightly on the table. I was immobile.

"Yeh think we'd rat out our own members?" Jenna said. "Yeh were so confident coming in here and asking questions. I bet yeh made a trash cop in America."

My gut twisted at her insult.

Was the driver still watching through the window? Could he see this far back into the salon? I should have let him come inside. What if one of them had a weapon?

I stopped squirming. "What do you want from me?"

Jenna laughed. "I think you already know what we want."

"You want me to break up with Seamus and leave Ireland? Well, I won't. You can't scare me."

"Is that so?" Jenna asked. "We could easily kill you right here. Finish the job others have failed to complete."

"I thought the ASB was a peaceful organization."

"Some of us are," the masseuse said with laughter in her voice. "Some of us aren't. We lean toward the less peaceful side."

"If you kill me, everyone will know it was you," I said. "Are you really ready to go to jail for killing someone over a man you have no chance with?"

The masseuse pushed me harder into the table. "You don't know who might have had a chance with him if you hadn't come into the picture, you money hungry—"

Jenna made the mistake of loosening her grip on my hands. I reached behind me, grabbed the masseuse's head, and yanked forward.

She toppled over the side of me and onto the floor.

I hurried to my feet, snatched up my purse, and ran out of the salon.

Before the driver could open the door, I did it myself and practically toppled into the car.

"What happened in there?" he asked.

"They were threatening me," I said. "But it's no big—"

He didn't wait for me to finish the sentence. He closed

the door, locked the car with the key fob in his pocket, and stormed into the salon.

I watched, my breathing shallow in my chest and tears trickling down my cheeks.

When he returned and slipped casually into the driver's seat, all he said was, "They won't be giving yeh trouble again."

I wanted to know what he'd done but knew he probably wouldn't tell me.

"Are yeh okay?" he asked.

"I'm fine. I just want to go home."

One glance at my nails sent tears streaming down my face again.

On each of my fingers was a hot pink, sloppily painted letter that spelled L-E-A-V-E-O-R-D-I-E.

"Leave or die," I whispered to myself. "Not a chance."

30

As if the day couldn't get any worse, in the cottage's driveway was a guarda car with its lights flashing, surrounded by angry-looking people holding signs that said awful things about me.

"Don't get out until I open yer door," the driver instructed. "I won't let anything happen to yeh."

I had a feeling what was about to happen to me would be out of his control.

Molly hurried to meet us and practically shouted, "Shayla Murphy, you're under arrest for murder." The rest of her spiel was drowned out by cheers from the group.

She gently escorted me to the garda car and helped me into the backseat. More smartphones than I could count were pointed at me, recording my every move.

I kept my head down and my mouth shut. There was no way I'd give them the satisfaction of my tears or shouts. If they wanted to dig up dirt on me, they'd have to do it the hard way.

Molly started down the drive toward the main road before she spoke.

"Listen carefully," Molly said. "Yer not actually under arrest. There is no evidence yeh killed or tried to kill anyone. The video on that site is false information, and we're doing our best to get to the bottom of it."

My heart raced at this revelation.

I wasn't actually going to jail?

Molly believed me?

"At the main road, I'll stop and quickly let yeh out of the car. You will get into the black SUV with tinted windows, and they will take yeh back to yer house when everyone has cleared out."

"What about the handcuffs?"

"They have a key to get them off," she said. "Someone else—a lookalike guarda officer—will get in the car in your place, and we will take her down to the station to keep up appearances."

"And then what?" I asked. "I just hide forever? There's no way you'll be able to find them all. They're everywhere, even at the nail salon. And most of them haven't committed any crimes. They're always going to hate me."

She glanced in the rearview mirror. "Do yeh love Seamus?"

"Yes," I said, without having to think about it.

"Even with all the knowledge yeh have about him? With the fact that he has a child and that he's wealthy and that people will hate yeh?"

"Yes," I said. "Nothing will keep me from loving him."

"Then don't give up on him. Trust me, you'll regret it."

The empathy I felt for her twisted with a weird kind of

jealousy, though I knew Seamus was wholeheartedly in love with me.

"We're almost there," she said. "No one is behind me yet, but they will be soon. Are yeh ready?"

"As I'll ever be," I said.

She slammed on the brakes, my head nearly banging into the seat in front of me.

When she flung open the door and pulled me out, another woman slipped in on the other side of the car and gave me a quick smile. She definitely looked like me.

The door to the black SUV was open, and Seamus jumped out to help me into the back seat.

"Thanks, Molly," he said before jumping in behind me.

She nodded and slammed the door before returning to her own car.

The SUV sped off up a different driveway that led to the stables and turned a corner just as a rush of vehicles came down the driveway. They all turned and followed Molly's car.

"I can't believe that worked," I said.

"Let me help you with those cuffs," Seamus said.

I turned away to give him my hands, and he quickly relieved me of the metal bracelets. I rubbed my wrists as I spun back around to face him.

"What in the name of everything holy is this?" he asked, looking at my nails.

"I had a little run-in at the nail salon," I said. "The driver took care of it."

"I'll be having a chat with Molly about this. This is a threat. They should be in jail."

"Thank you for all this," I said, trying to change the

subject. I wasn't exactly proud of how I'd handled the nail salon incident. I'd stupidly put myself in danger, then run away like a damsel in distress instead of confronting them as a proper police officer would have.

"Don't thank me," he said. "This was all Molly's idea. I wanted to whisk yeh off back to America, but she said we should stay put. She's convinced this will blow over the moment she solves the cases."

"I went to see Patricia," I said. "Mostly to see if her nails were pink since whoever put the poison in my drink had pink nails."

"Were they?"

"No," I said. "But her assistant's were freshly painted."

"That's why yeh went to the nail salon."

"They knew who I was straight away. I was so stupid to think I was being sneaky. But they did give away one useful tidbit—the assistant is part of the ASB which means she likely could have tried to poison my drink."

"Along with apparently every other pink-nailed person in Ireland."

He was right. I'd gotten nowhere. Except about the cameras. "You know the guy we saw last night that ran into that house?"

"The old one who almost called the Gardaí on us?"

"That's the one," I said. "Except he's not old—that was a disguise. He's probably around our age, and he's the one who's been following me."

"Maybe he's the one who tried to kill yeh."

I slowly shook my head. "I don't think so. He didn't have pink nails, for one." I waited for Seamus to laugh, but he apparently didn't find my imminent peril amusing. "And he gave me a tip about the castle cameras."

"I thought the cameras were offline that day."

"He said there are two different sections of cameras—the ones to protect the castle and the ones to watch the staff—we need to check the ones that watch the staff."

"We should tell Molly about it," Seamus said. "She'll be able to get the footage and solve the case."

His confidence in Molly's ability, paired with Molly's obvious regret for letting Seamus go, made my chest tighten with jealousy. I pushed it away. Molly would be in our lives forever. Either I needed to trust Seamus completely, or I needed to return to America like the ASB wanted.

"I sent Telly a text," I said. "But she hasn't replied."

"Have yeh tried to call her?"

I hadn't, but it didn't hurt to try.

I pulled out my phone and called the number but reached a disconnect message. "Sounds like she changed her number."

"It's okay. Everything will work out," Seamus said, wrapping an arm around me and pulling me to his chest.

The driver parked the SUV behind the cottage in the dark. After what felt like forever, we were finally led through the dark into the cottage.

31

The driver told us he'd be outside if we needed anything before closing the doors. Seamus turned all the locks—locks that hadn't been there when I'd left earlier in the day.

"Can I turn on the lights?" I asked. "Or will they see us?"

"We had security blackouts installed over the windows," Seamus said. "They're bulletproof and won't give away the fact that we're inside."

"How did you get everything done so quickly?" I asked.

"Milton wanted a way to make it up to us that he had ASB members on his crew. He did all of this in record time."

I flipped on the light and nearly screamed when I saw someone standing in the middle of the kitchen staring at us.

"Shhh," Telly said, glancing around as if someone outside might hear me if I screamed. "I thought you had been arrested. I just came by to see if Seamus needed my help freeing you. I found some information, but I can go if you—"

"How did yeh get in the house?" Seamus asked.

"Don't worry. I have an extraordinary ability to pick locks. It took me a while, but there was plenty of distraction out front to give me all the time I needed."

Seamus looked slightly frightened by her. "I'll be in my office if yeh need anything. Magella is planning on bringing dinner in about a half hour."

"How sweet of her," I said. "I'll let you know when she arrives."

He left Telly and me standing in awkward silence.

"Sorry I bolted out of here this morning," Telly said, her hands shoved deep into her pockets.

"I understand," I said. "I mean, I don't really, but it's okay. But you don't have to worry about me. I'm not a police officer anymore, and your past is of no interest to me unless it will affect me."

She considered this for a moment. "It should not affect you."

"Great," I said. "Now that we've settled that, shall we get down to business?"

Telly smiled. "Let's do it."

She moved into the living room, slipped off her shoes, and sat cross-legged on the couch, pulling her laptop into her lap.

I sat next to her and watched as she typed and clicked faster than my brain could register.

"I found the camera footage you referenced in your text," she said. "They're not great angles, but the quality is exceptional. Whoever is in charge at that castle really wants to keep an eye on their staff."

"Can we start with the day Claudine was pushed?"

She typed and clicked and a video appeared. "This is from the valet station."

The video mainly showed the podium where the valets stood and the keys were housed, but in the frame's corner, you could see the edge of the steps leading to the castle doors.

We watched from the moment the sun came up as the staff slowly trickled in. Patricia arrived first, with Anna and Freya coming in behind her dressed in white assistant uniforms.

A single valet arrived, then Claudine and Roland, Seamus and me, and—after a bit—the gardaí.

"Did you see anyone leave before the gardaí arrived?" I asked Telly.

"I don't think so, but I can go back." She pulled the little red dot to the left and then pressed play.

We watched as the valet checked and rechecked the cleanliness of the podium, but the entire time not a single person walked down those steps and into the parking lot.

I was pretty sure Patricia had told Molly she sent Freya home. She said Freya had been hysterical or something, which was what I'd witnessed when Patricia seemed to be trying to calm her down.

Did Patricia know at that moment that Freya pushed Claudine? If so, wouldn't she have been angrier at Freya?

"We need to get an angle of the back of the hotel," I said. "Maybe we can see when and how Freya goes over the cliff."

Telly went through several other recordings, but none showed the back of the castle.

"Dang," I said, flopping back on the couch. "What about the one on the side of the castle? Maybe we'll get lucky and see someone go around that way."

She went back to the recording and pressed play.

"We can probably skip forward to just before the gardaí arrived. That's when Patricia said she told Freya to go home."

When the time stamp was correct, she pushed play again, and we watched.

Sure enough, about two minutes later, Freya walked around the side of the castle, wiping tears from her eyes.

"Let's keep watching and see if anyone follows her," I said. If Patricia came around the side of the castle toward the cliffs, I'd be able to give Molly a slightly better reason to arrest Patricia. However, proving Patricia pushed Freya over the cliff would still be difficult.

Either way, it didn't matter because Patricia never walked around this side of the castle, and Freya didn't walk back.

"What do you think?" Telly asked, setting her laptop on the coffee table.

"I feel like there's more going on regarding these deaths. But there's no way to prove any of it."

"You don't think she jumped off the cliff?"

I shook my head. "No, but who knows? It's possible that she felt remorseful after pushing Claudine over the rail, especially if she thought Claudine was me and nearly killed the wrong person."

A knock at the door interrupted my thought process.

Seamus appeared within seconds. "It's Magella and Mam. I saw them arrive on the cameras." He unlocked the door and took several of the bags from Magella's hands.

"Oh my gosh, Shayla, are you okay?" Gráinne dropped all her bags on the counter and rushed to my side, wrapping her arms around me and squeezing.

"I've had better days, that's for sure," I said.

She picked up one of my hands and said, "We brought remover to get this off. How horrible they did that to yeh. Trust me. They'll be out of business in no time."

"Because they'll be in jail," Seamus added.

Telly shrunk back against the couch, keeping her head lowered. I considered introducing her to Magella and Gráinne but didn't want to invade her privacy.

While Gráinne went to work on my nails, Magella started setting our small kitchen table.

"Can I help you with anything?" Telly asked, walking to the kitchen.

Magella put her straight to work without asking who she was.

"Is that Telly?" Gráinne whispered.

I nodded, not wanting Telly to catch on that we were talking about her.

"Seamus told me about her."

Was she going to tell me not to bring random people onto the property? Even though I knew practically nothing about Telly, she was the first person in Ireland besides Seamus and his family to whom I felt a kinship. Maybe it was because we were both from America. Maybe it was something else.

"I'm glad yeh have a friend," Gráinne finally said. "Friends are so important in life."

Every bit of me wanted to throw my arms around her neck and hug her forever.

"There, that's better." She gave me back my hands, now free of all disturbing nail polish.

"Food's ready," Magella said.

"How's the filly doing?" Seamus asked when we were all happily munching on the roast beef and mashed potatoes.

"She's grand," Gráinne said, her face lighting up. "I'm so pleased she made it."

"Have you named her yet?" I asked.

"Not yet," Gráinne said. "Do you have any thoughts?"

"Me?" I asked.

Gráinne laughed. "If you'd like, absolutely. There are plenty of foals born for everyone to take a turn naming them."

I considered this for a moment. She needed the perfect name, not just a random name like Buttercup. Not that there was anything wrong with the name Buttercup.

"You don't have to come up with something right now," Seamus said, squeezing my knee.

"I'll think about it and get back to you, okay?"

"We're in no rush," Gráinne said.

"Oh, that's my phone." Seamus pulled his buzzing phone from his pocket. He looked at the screen and frowned. "I should probably take this." He stood from the table and started toward the living room. "Hello?"

Gráinne and I exchanged a confused shrug. Telly looked like a scared cat, ready to bolt at any moment.

Magella was the only one who didn't seem concerned about the call taking place in hushed tones just a few feet from us.

"What's wrong?" I asked when Seamus returned to the table.

"Someone ran Molly's car off the road on her way to the station. They assume whoever did it was trying to hurt you because they thought yeh were in the back."

Panic rushed through me. "Is Molly okay?"

"She's at the hospital," Seamus said. "But she's expected to be just fine."

"And the woman in the back seat?"

Seamus shook his head. "They ran right into her door. The car crumpled. She's in bad shape."

Dizziness overtook me. That would have been me. And because it wasn't me, someone else—the woman pretending to be me—could die.

"This has to stop," I said. "We need to figure out who is doing this."

Telly and I both stood at the same time.

"I'll look deeper into the ASB," she said. "Maybe I can figure out who the leader is, and we can get them to call off the dogs."

"Do you think we should go to the hospital to check on Molly?" I asked Seamus.

He shook his head. "Right now, we want the ASB members to think they succeeded with their plan."

Telly was typing and clicking faster than she had been before as Gráinne and Magella began cleaning up dinner.

It seemed we'd all lost our appetites.

32

I must have fallen asleep, hypnotized by Telly's frantic typing and clicking. When I woke, I had to check my phone for the time because the blackout shades kept the sun completely out.

"Good afternoon, sleepyhead," Telly said from the same position as where I'd seen her before closing my eyes.

"Did you find anything?" My voice was raspy, and I was sure my hair was a complete disaster.

She shook her head. "Not yet, but I'm getting closer."

Seamus was asleep in the chair on the other side of the coffee table. Gráinne and Magella must have gone after cleaning the kitchen.

"I can't believe I fell asleep. Have you been up the entire time?"

Telly shrugged. "I just need to figure this out."

"Coffee?"

"Love some."

I stood and stretched, my back and neck aching from my sleeping position on the couch. "Cream? Sugar?"

"Just black," Telly said.

I brewed a pot and doctored mine with plenty of cream and sugar before taking our mugs back to the couch.

I had just sat down when a knock at the back door nearly made me spill hot coffee down my front.

Seamus was on his feet before his eyes had even opened. "Don't open the door," he whispered. "I'll check the cameras."

"It's me—Molly." The voice came through the door, but Seamus insisted on checking to ensure it was Molly before we let her in. When he nodded, I unlocked all the locks.

Molly stood on the other side, looking pretty banged up but alive. I resisted the urge to hug her.

"Don't hug me," Molly said as if she could see my thoughts through my eyes.

"I wasn't," I said with a laugh.

"How's your colleague?" Seamus asked.

I turned back to look at him and realized Telly had disappeared from the couch. She'd taken her computer and backpack with her.

"She's still in critical condition, but we're holding out hope."

"Coffee?" I asked Molly.

"I've already had several cups," Molly said. "But sure, why not?"

"Seamus?" I asked.

"Thanks, love."

I brought them each their mugs along with sugar and cream on the table for Molly in case she used it.

"Did something come up in the case?" I asked when we were all cozy with our drinks.

"That's not why I'm here," Molly said, staring down into her mug. "I have something I need to tell yeh."

My stomach dropped. This was it. She was going to tell him.

I stood and moved to sit on the arm of Seamus' chair.

He gave me a confused look, then turned his attention back to Molly. "We're all ears."

"There's no easy way to say this, so I'm just going to say it. Seamus, yeh have a daughter. We have a daughter."

Seamus's shoulder muscles tensed under my arm, but he said nothing.

Neither of them did. For a long time.

The silence was practically killing me, but this was not my time to speak. This was between the two of them. Of course, I'd be part of it too, but that was not at the forefront of this conversation.

Seamus finally cleared his throat. "Yeh didn't lose the baby?"

Molly shook her head. "I thought I had, but when I returned home, I realized I was still with child."

"Why didn't yeh tell me?" Seamus's accent thickened along with his building emotions.

"I didn't want yeh to think I was only in it for the money."

"That would mean she's—"

"Six," Molly said. "She has yer eyes."

"Six years? I've missed six years? How could yeh do

this to me, Molls? Yeh knew how badly I wanted to be a daddy."

Tears stung my eyes. I could almost feel the sadness radiating off him.

"At first, I was angry," Molly said. "Then, as time passed and yeh didn't come back, I just thought it was for the best. I didn't want to make yer decisions for yeh."

Seamus took a couple of deep breaths. I'd only seen him this worked up a handful of times.

Finally, he said, "What's her name?"

"Lila," Molly said. "Lila Jane Ryan."

"Can I meet her?"

Even though I suspected Molly had been preparing herself for this question, she still seemed surprised by it. "O'course yeh can."

"I'm happy to pay whatever support owed for the past six years and the years going forward," Seamus said.

I was so proud of how he was taking this. He was so calm and level-headed.

"Yeh don't need to be doin' that," Molly said. "We've made it just fine this far."

"It's me responsibility," Seamus said. "I'd also like to build a relationship with her."

Another wave of surprise crossed Molly's face. "O'course."

"Where is she now?" Seamus asked. "Where'd she go last night when yeh were in the hospital?"

"One of me officers has girls around her age," Molly said. "She took Lila for the night."

"I bet she was worried about yeh," Seamus said.

"We FaceTimed."

The conversation dropped into another silence. Though this one was more awkward.

Molly's phone rang from her purse, and she hesitantly pulled it out. "Ah, I have to go. Can we talk about this again later?"

Seamus, Molly, and I stood and walked to the door.

"Let's set a time when we can meet her," Seamus said, squeezing my hand.

Molly looked from Seamus to me, then back again. "We'll do that." She flashed me a quick smile before walking out the door.

Seamus turned to me and practically melted in my embrace. "I'm so sorry, Shay. I had no idea."

"You don't have to apologize to me," I said. "I'm sorry you've missed so many years."

Seamus straightened up. "I can't believe she'd do something so horrible. That's my child too. My daughter." His voice was elevated to almost a full yell. "She should have told me the moment she knew she hadn't lost the baby. Who cares if we'd split up?"

I rubbed a hand down his back. "I know. It's a terrible secret to have kept."

He turned to me. "How are you so calm about all of this?"

"I'm not. It's a lot to take in."

His eyes searched mine. "Yeh already knew, didn't yeh?"

"No," I said. "Well, yes. But only for a couple of days. I saw them at the hospital, and she has your eyes. There was no mistaking. And Molly made me promise not to say anything."

"I can't believe yeh didn't tell meh," Seamus yelled.

"I'm not the bad guy here," I said, my voice increasingly irritated. "This wasn't my secret to tell."

"I thought we were supposed to tell each other everything."

"That's not fair," I said. "You know everything about me. I'm not the one known to keep secrets."

Seamus gaped at me.

"I'm sorry, that wasn't fair." If only I could take back what I'd said.

"Yer right," Seamus said. "I'm the liar here. Yer perfect."

"That's not what I said." Angry tears sprung to my eyes.

"I need some air." Seamus walked out the door, slamming it behind him.

33

I flopped down on the couch and opened the notes app on my phone to jot down everything going through my mind.

"Is the coast clear?" Telly asked, coming back into the room.

I nearly fell off the couch. I'd forgotten she was still there.

"Are you okay?" Telly asked.

I cleared my throat of as much emotion as possible. "I'm fine."

She nodded and didn't push any further.

"Have you found anything?"

"There's a password-protected part of the ASB site, and behind it is enough evidence to put what seems like the entire group in prison. The only problem is, the members never speak to one another using their real names."

"Can we track their individual computer logins?"

"We can," Telly said slowly. "But it would take hours to track them all down."

"Do you know who the leader of the site is? The one who uploaded the new video?"

"I don't know who, but I can find out where."

"Perfect," I said. "Then we can confront them."

A smile formed on Telly's lips. "And bring them to justice."

I flipped to my photos app and started going through all the photos I'd taken of the crime scene. Maybe there was something I'd missed.

It was hard to see Claudine, with her blonde ringlets and tear-streaked face lying on the stone floor. Maybe she did look a bit like me.

As I flipped onto other photos, one caught my eye. The one of the smudge on Claudine's white shirt. I zoomed in but couldn't figure out what it would have been from.

"What's that?" Telly asked, looking over my shoulder.

I handed her the phone, and she examined the photo. "It looks like words."

"Words?" I asked. "Can you tell what it says?"

She shook her head and handed it back to me. Maybe it's a tattoo that's just showing up from beneath her white shirt?

"It was definitely a stain on the shirt itself," I said. Then a thought occurred to me. I went into a photo editing app and flipped the photo, so it was a mirror image of itself. "Look at that."

Telly squinted. "What does it say?"

"DO IT NOW," I said. "Why would the words DO IT NOW be stained backward on Claudine's shirt?"

"I think I figured out where the user uploaded the video." Telly turned the computer to face me. A small red dot was right in the middle of Ballywick. As she zoomed in, the location became even clearer—the back of the nail salon.

My heart twisted. Could the person responsible for all this be one of the women who'd attacked me at the salon?

"We have to get over there," I said, trying to get to my feet.

Telly grabbed my arm and pulled me back to the couch. "Not so fast. It would be no use storming the castle when we're not confident the user is there."

"Will we know in real-time when they're there?"

Telly nodded. "But if we're going to confront them, we need to get into town without being recognized. Everyone thinks you're in a hospital bed fighting for your life, right?"

That answered my question about whether she'd been listening from wherever she'd gone off to when Molly arrived. "Right."

"And if you magically show up, they will come at you with pitchforks and flaming torches again, right?"

I chuckled a bit at the thought.

"Metaphorically," Telly said.

"Right."

"So you need a disguise."

"Like a hat to cover my hair?"

Telly reached into her backpack and pulled out two different wigs. "Do you want to be a ginger or a brunette?"

I chose the short red-headed wig, and Telly expertly

tied my curls up and pinned the wig on so it wasn't going anywhere. My gut told me she had more experience in disguise than most people, but I'd promised not to pry.

A notification dinged on her computer.

"Looks like it's time to go," she said.

"How are we going to get there?" I asked. "We can't take one of the cars—they won't drive me off the property."

"I called a cab," she said. "They're going to pull up to the back."

She'd thought of everything.

We slipped in as quickly and quietly as possible when the cab pulled up.

While Telly told the driver where to take us, I sent a text to Seamus telling him where I'd gone and that I'd be back soon.

When my phone dinged with a reply almost instantly, I assumed it would be Seamus. Instead, it was Molly.

Do you recognize this earring?

A photo of a pink feather earring popped up beneath her text.

patricia was wearing some like it the day claudine fell. why?

It was clutched in Freya's hand.

My mind raced. Did that mean Patricia had pushed her over the cliff? Then something came to me.

was anything written on Freya's left hand

No. Her hands seemed to have been scrubbed clean before she went over the edge.

patricia did this

We need hard evidence. The earring is a start. I'm at the hospital right now. Claudine has been recovering quickly. They think she'll be conscious soon.

The cab pulled to a stop.

Telly paid the driver as I returned my phone to my pocket. If Patricia were the one behind the computer, we'd have all the evidence we needed.

elly led me around the back of Ballywick Nails, where a stairway led below ground to a basement entrance.

On the door, a sign said: *Sensuous Silver Syndicate.*

"What does that mean?" Telly asked, pointing at the sign.

"Well, hello," a voice said from above us.

I glanced up, shielding my eyes from the sun, to see Seamus's Aunt Shannon.

She walked down the stairs and knocked on the door three times slowly, then twice quickly. "Are you ladies here for book club?" She didn't seem to recognize me.

The door swung open to a cozy room full of women's faces and surrounded by wall-to-wall bookshelves filled with thousands of books.

"Yep," I said. "Here to discuss some books."

Telly looked like she might pass out. She tried to turn back, but more women were making their way down the stairs, all carrying the same book with the bare-chested man that both Patricia and Margaret had been reading.

And when I surveyed the room, Patricia and Margaret were in the group, though sitting as far from one another as possible in the small space.

"Come in," one of the women with pure silver hair said. "We're happy to see the new faces. Don't be shy. Take a seat."

We sat as far in the back as possible.

I tried to see if Patricia was on a computer or had a computer close to her, but I couldn't see anything through the group.

"Shall we *slide* right into the book?" the woman with silver hair asked.

"Maybe we should all introduce ourselves since we have new members," Margaret said.

Telly stiffened beside me.

"Ooh, what a good idea. I'll start. I'm Niamh," the woman with silver hair said. "I started the group a few years ago. Margaret, would you like to go next?"

"I'm Margaret Carragher." The way she said her name matched her tough and dignified personality.

The women went around saying their names, Patricia barely looking up from whatever she was doing to speak. I suspected she was doing something on the ASB site, but there was no way to prove it without Telly's computer.

When the introductions came around to Telly, I stood instead. "My name is Shayla Murphy. I'm not here to talk about a book. I'm here to talk about murder."

Patricia nearly dropped the small laptop I could now see perched on her knees.

"Shayla?" Shannon said. "What happened to your hair?"

"Don't tell me you're here to relay some ridiculous story about me trying to murder Claudine," Margaret said. "The gardaí have officially cleared me."

"Nope," I said. "Not you. Patricia is responsible for not only Claudine's fall but the murders of both Freya and Kellan."

Patricia narrowed her eyes at me while her assistant next to her shifted nervously in her seat.

"Everyone knows you did it," Patricia said. "We just thought you were dead too."

"Nope, the person your members tried to kill—yes tried, she's not dead—was an undercover guarda officer."

"Anna, call the Gardaí and tell them Shayla Murphy is here for them to arrest," Patricia told her assistant.

The woman didn't miss a beat before doing exactly what Patricia asked.

"Is that all you had to do to get her to put poison in my drink that night?" I asked. "Are the members so brainwashed by you and your deceased boyfriend they'll literally murder for you?"

"What members?" Patricia said, but her voice was changing slightly. "You keep saying members, and I have no idea what you're talking about."

Telly stood next to me. "My guess is if I opened your computer, I'd find out your username is Pink Pink Pink."

I gaped at Telly. If she'd told me the username was Pink Pink Pink, I'd have known exactly who was to blame.

"My computer is private property," Patricia said, hugging it to her chest as Telly inched back into her seat.

"Did you do it?" Margaret asked. "Did you try to kill Claudine?"

"What do you care what happened to Claudine?" Patricia spat. "Not that I did it, but you have no right to act like you're upset about her getting hurt."

"Oh, and you do?" Margaret laughed. "You act like you and Claudine were the best of friends. But you barely knew Claudine before they started planning their wedding at the castle. Which makes me wonder—why have you been spending so much time at her bedside? Perhaps to make sure she doesn't talk when she wakes up? I can't believe I didn't see it before."

"If that's the case," I said. "It's too late. Claudine is likely waking up as we speak. Then she's going to tell us exactly what happened."

"Freya pushed her then jumped over the cliff out of guilt," Patricia said. "That's what happened."

"Nice try," I said. "But when Freya grabbed Claudine to push her over the edge, the note you wrote on her hand transferred to Claudine's shirt. In the same black ink you used to write something on Anna's hand, you wrote DO IT NOW on Freya's. Which likely meant she was supposed to push me over the edge, but she picked the wrong blonde. That's why she was hyperventilating. You were trying to calm her down, and when you couldn't, you pushed her over the edge. My guess is that she was going to go to the Gardaí and confess."

"I want to see you prove this," Patricia said. "Any of it. It's absurd."

"Is it absurd that they found one of your pink feather earrings in Freya's hand when they brought her in for the autopsy?"

The other women gasped.

"Do you want to show us your ears? If one of your earrings were yanked out, it would have ripped your earlobe."

Patricia stood. "I'm not showing you anything. You're not a guarda. You're nothing but a gold-digging American who needs to leave well enough alone."

"Do the other members of the ASB know you're willing to kill your own if they catch on to you? Does Anna know she could be next?"

Anna turned back, still on the phone with the Gardaí, and stared wide-eyed at Patricia.

"It must be horrible to live with the guilt that your instructions killed your boyfriend," I said gently. "He was supposed to be at home, wasn't he? You didn't know he'd be at the pub."

Patricia's face reddened with emotion. "It was supposed to be you," she whispered. "Why won't you just die?"

She jolted toward me, her hands outstretched, reaching for my neck.

But before she could reach me, Shannon stood up and punched Patricia square in the face. Patricia went down hard on the floor, completely unconscious.

The room was silent for a split second before all the women cheered.

I slid back into my seat, and Telly handed me my phone. "I recorded the entire thing."

The gardaí arrived shortly after and took Patricia and Anna into custody.

"That was good work," Margaret said, standing next to me. "If you ever need a job, let me know."

"A job doing what?" I asked.

"This and that." Margaret winked and walked away.

"Shannon, that was a brilliant punch," I said.

"I KO'd her," Shannon said, a bit of awe in her voice. "I couldn't let her attack you."

"Thank you," I said, giving her a quick hug.

"I should be the one thanking you for taking care of Killian the other night," she said.

"It was no big deal," I said. "And Seamus did all the heavy lifting."

She laughed. "I'm glad you'll be joining the family. And come back to book club anytime. That was grand."

"We should probably head home," I said to Telly.

"There are still ASB members who probably want me dead. And news of my being alive will be spread far and wide within the hour."

Telly nodded, and we pushed through the crowd and out to the stairwell.

"Jaysus, Mary, and Joseph." Seamus stood at the top of the steps. "I can't leave yeh alone for an afternoon without yeh getting yerself into trouble, can I?"

"I sent you a message," I said.

He held out his arms. "I'm so sorry I was harsh. I shouldn't have taken my frustration with Molly out on you."

I hurried up the stairs and hugged him. "I'm sorry too. I should have told you the moment I found out."

"Uh, hi," a man said from behind me. "Have you seen Margaret?"

I turned to find Finn standing off to the side of the stairwell. He may have been asking me the question, but his eyes were solidly focused on Telly.

"She just left," I said. "I thought you were a PI. Shouldn't you have seen her?"

"I can't be all places at once." He smiled at Telly, but she just looked away. "I was at the hospital. Claudine is awake."

"We should go see her," I said to Seamus, then turned back to invite Telly to go with us, but she was gone.

"She went that way," Finn said. "Not that I was watching or anything."

"Let's go," Seamus said.

The hospital was packed with people wanting to talk to Claudine. Molly was still in the room, probably taking her official statement when we arrived to find a hallway full of people.

I overheard Roland talking to Margaret as we approached.

"You don't have to be here," he said.

She reached into her purse. "I can tell she means a lot to you. Why don't you give her this?"

"But—"

"Just take it before I change my mind," Margaret said.

Roland didn't take the ring box but wrapped his mother in a giant bear hug, lifting her off the ground.

She laughed and then smoothed her clothes when he put her down. "Don't you ever do that again."

Roland shook his head. "Always so serious."

She smiled at him.

"We'd also like to give you your wedding date back," I said.

Seamus and I had talked about it in the car. We'd be able to find a different date, especially since Patricia had been lying to us the entire time.

The door to Claudine's room opened, and Roland rushed inside as Molly walked out.

"Care to fill me in with what happened at book club?" Molly asked, grabbing me by the crook of my arm and pulling me toward the elevator.

"But we were going to see Claudine."

"You'll be waiting a while," Molly said. "Let's get some dinner and discuss things."

I glanced at Seamus, who nodded.

"We can do that," I said as we stepped into the elevator. "What did Claudine say?"

"She said she and Roland argued, and as she was looking over the edge, someone grabbed her by the hair and left arm and whispered in her ear something like leave Seamus alone and go back where you came from."

"That would explain her saying what are you talking about."

Molly nodded. "I hear you got video of Patricia confessing?"

"I'll send it to you," I said. "Where should we go to dinner?"

"How about the two of you come to my place, we'll order pizza, and you can meet Lila?" Molly's voice shook as she spoke.

Seamus glanced at me to see what I thought.

I smiled.

"That would be wonderful," Seamus said.

"Can we bring anything?" I asked.

"You could pick up pizzas from the pizzeria in town," Molly said. "That'll give me enough time to prepare Lila for what's to come."

I swallowed back the emotion welling up in my chest. Seamus was about to meet his daughter. Did I even have a right to be there? Maybe I needed to let the three of them do this without me.

"I can just go back to the cottage if you think—"

"No," Molly interrupted me. "You'll be in Lila's life just as much as Seamus will. I want you to be there."

Seamus squeezed my hand. "So do I."

I stood a bit straighter and smiled. "All right then. What kind of pizza?"

"Margherita for us," Molly said.

"One Margherita and one Pepperoni then," Seamus said. "Send us the address and we'll be there once the pizza is ready."

"Do I look okay?" Seamus asked. He'd insisted we stop by the cottage before picking up the pizza and heading to Molly's house.

"You look great," I said, surveying his jeans and sweater look. "Approachable and kind, but not too serious. What about me?"

"Yeh look gorgeous in everything yeh wear," Seamus said. "But I think yeh look absolutely grand tonight."

I'd carefully fixed my hair into long French braids, swiped on a bit of extra mascara, and put on my favorite pair of jeans and a pretty pink blouse.

"Should we go?" I asked.

"Yes."

We drove in silence, hand-in-hand. I couldn't tell which of us was more nervous.

The pizzeria was adorable on the inside. Seamus tipped them heavily and slipped the pizzas into the back seat before starting toward the address Molly had texted him.

My mouth watered as the aroma of the pizzas hit my

nose. I was about to comment on how hungry I was to break the silence, but Seamus slowed the car so we could locate the correct house.

A small white terrace house between two other homes was theirs. The narrow front of the house had a single window on the main level next to a greenish-gray door. On the second level were two additional windows.

"This looks nice," I said as Seamus parallel parked the car on the street.

"It looks tiny," Seamus said. "But well-kept. Do yeh think I should offer to get her a new home? A bigger home?"

I shrugged. "That's up to you. But I'd give it some time. Get to know Lila and Molly as a mother. Money seemed to be a touchy subject."

Seamus sucked in a deep breath and gazed deeply into my eyes. "Thank yeh for being here with me. I don't know how I'd do this without yeh by my side. I hope yeh know this will change nothing between us."

His smile said he truly believed that. But I knew better.

This would change everything.

Get the next book in the Shayla Murphy series—*Muddy Murder*!

Also, I'd love it if you'd leave a review on Amazon/Goodreads/Bookbub!

. . .

I love hearing from readers! Email me at stellabixbyauthor@gmail.com or join my mailing list at www.stellabixby.com

ACKNOWLEDGMENTS

I am so thankful for my family, friends, and God. Their consistent encouragement and support is crucial to my productivity and process as an author.

My readers are everything. Without my readers, I'd be out of a job. Thank YOU so much for reading my books—I hope they have given you a bit of escape and joy.

A huge thanks to my beta readers, ARC readers, social media sharers, and fellow authors. You are all integral to my success.

ABOUT THE AUTHOR

Stella Bixby is a native Coloradan who loves to snowboard, pluck at the guitar, and play board games with her family. She was once a volunteer firefighter and a park ranger, but now spends most of her time making up stories and trying to figure out what to cook for dinner.

Connect with Stella on Facebook, Twitter, and Instagram @StellaBixby.

Stella loves to hear from her readers!
www.stellabixby.com

ALSO BY STELLA BIXBY

Novels:

Rylie Cooper Series

Catfished: Book 1

Suckered: Book 2

Throttled: Book 3

Tampered: Book 4

Whacked: Book 5

Bungled: Book 6

Snowed: Book 7

Wasted: Book 8

Booked: Book 9

Shayla Murphy Series

Mistletoe Malarkey: Book 1

Veiled Vengeance: Book 2

Magical Mane Mystery Series

Downward Death: Book 1

Bowling Blunder: Book 2

Spotlight Scandal: Book 3

Tango Trouble: Book 4

Spelunking Speculations: Book 5

Festival Fiasco: Book 6

Jamboree Justice: Book 7

9 781954 367166